WEREWOLF

Written and illustrated by
Jeff Zornow

visit us at
www.abdopublishing.com

Published by Magic Wagon, a division of the ABDO Publishing Group, 8000 West
78th Street, Edina, Minnesota 55439. Copyright © 2008 by Abdo Consulting
Group, Inc. International copyrights reserved in all countries. All rights reserved.
No part of this book may be reproduced in any form without written permission
from the publisher. Graphic Planet™ is a trademark and logo of Magic Wagon.

Printed in the United States.

Written and illustrated by Jeff Zornow
Colored and lettered by Jay Fotos
Edited & Directed by Chazz DeMoss
Cover Design by Neil Klinepier

Library of Congress Cataloging-in-Publication Data

Zornow, Jeff.
  Werewolf / written [by] Jeff Zornow.
     p. cm. -- (Graphic horror)
  ISBN-13: 978-1-60270-062-8
  1. Graphic novels. I. Title.
  PN6727.Z67W47 2008
  741.5'973--dc22

                                        2007016371

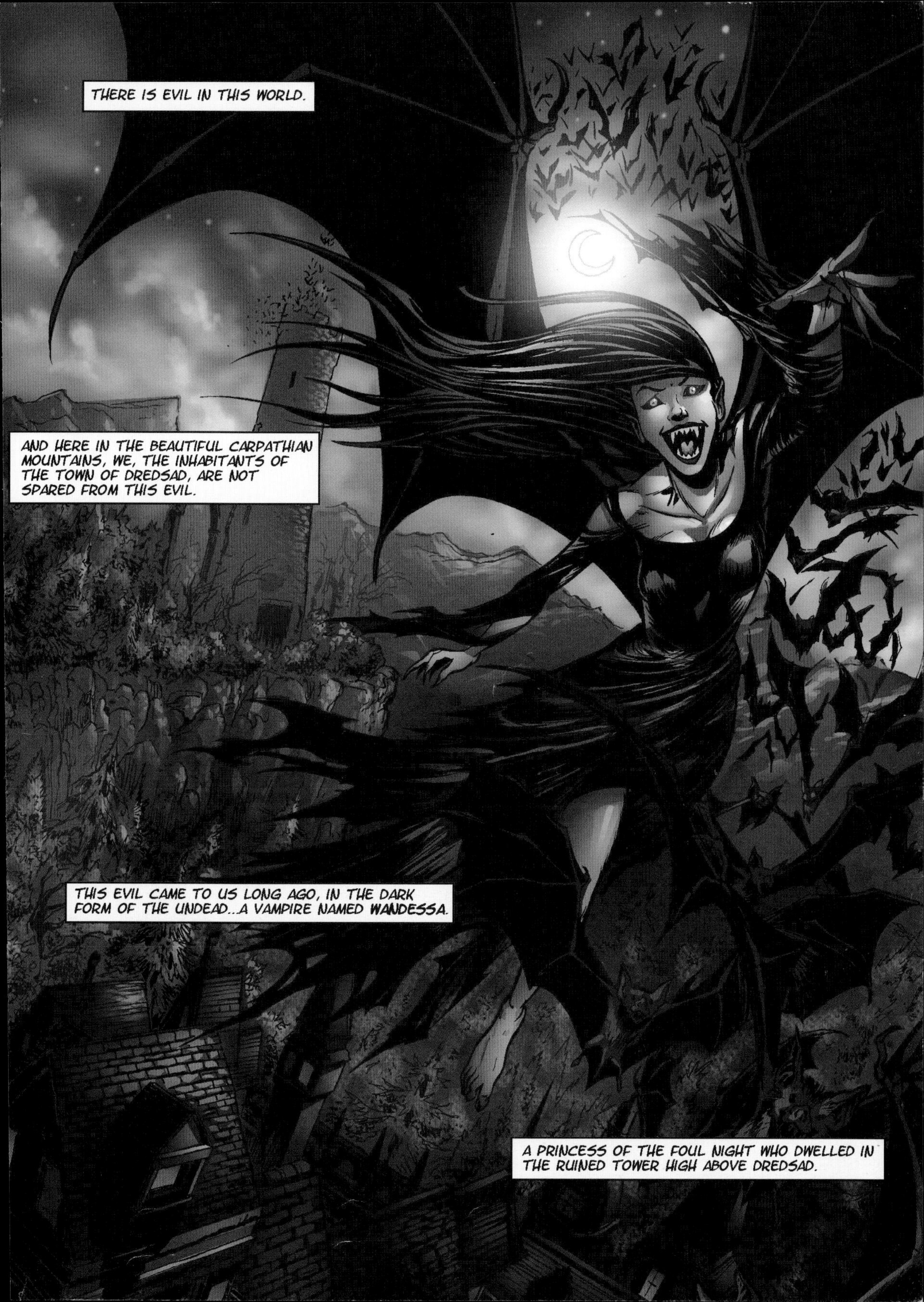
THERE IS EVIL IN THIS WORLD.
AND HERE IN THE BEAUTIFUL CARPATHIAN MOUNTAINS, WE, THE INHABITANTS OF THE TOWN OF DREDSAD, ARE NOT SPARED FROM THIS EVIL.
THIS EVIL CAME TO US LONG AGO, IN THE DARK FORM OF THE UNDEAD...A VAMPIRE NAMED WANDESSA.
A PRINCESS OF THE FOUL NIGHT WHO DWELLED IN THE RUINED TOWER HIGH ABOVE DREDSAD.

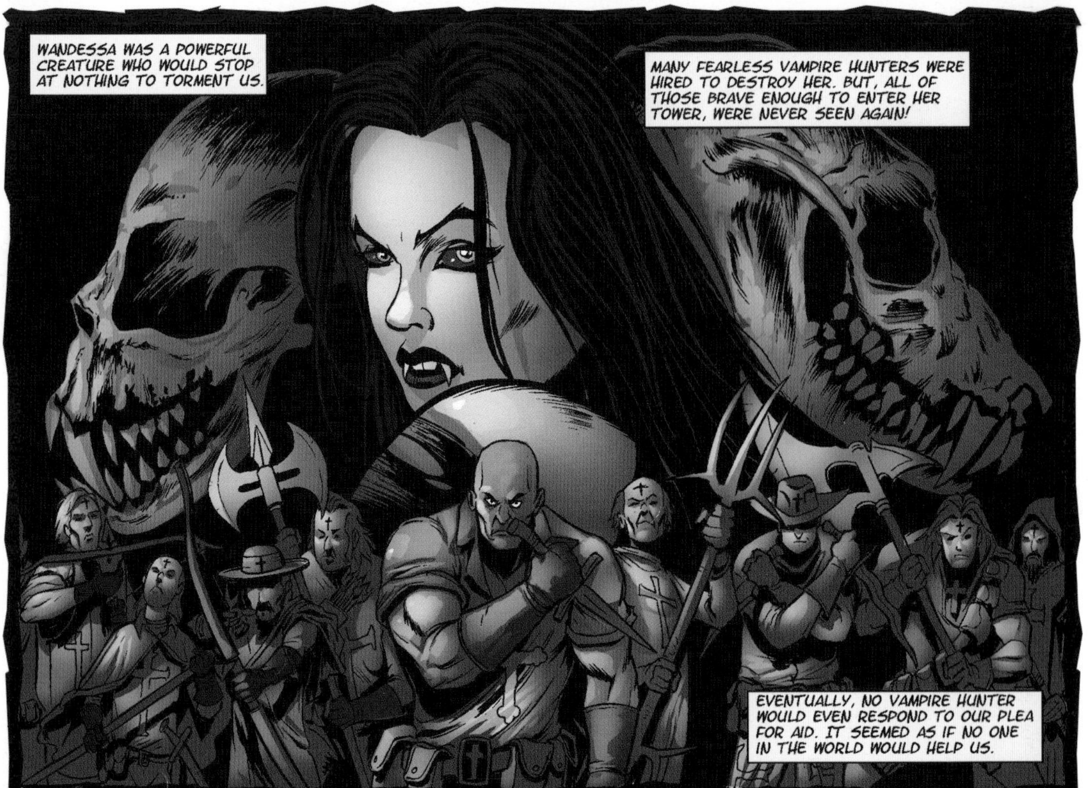
WANDESSA WAS A POWERFUL CREATURE WHO WOULD STOP AT NOTHING TO TORMENT US.
MANY FEARLESS VAMPIRE HUNTERS WERE HIRED TO DESTROY HER. BUT, ALL OF THOSE BRAVE ENOUGH TO ENTER HER TOWER, WERE NEVER SEEN AGAIN!
EVENTUALLY, NO VAMPIRE HUNTER WOULD EVEN RESPOND TO OUR PLEA FOR AID. IT SEEMED AS IF NO ONE IN THE WORLD WOULD HELP US.

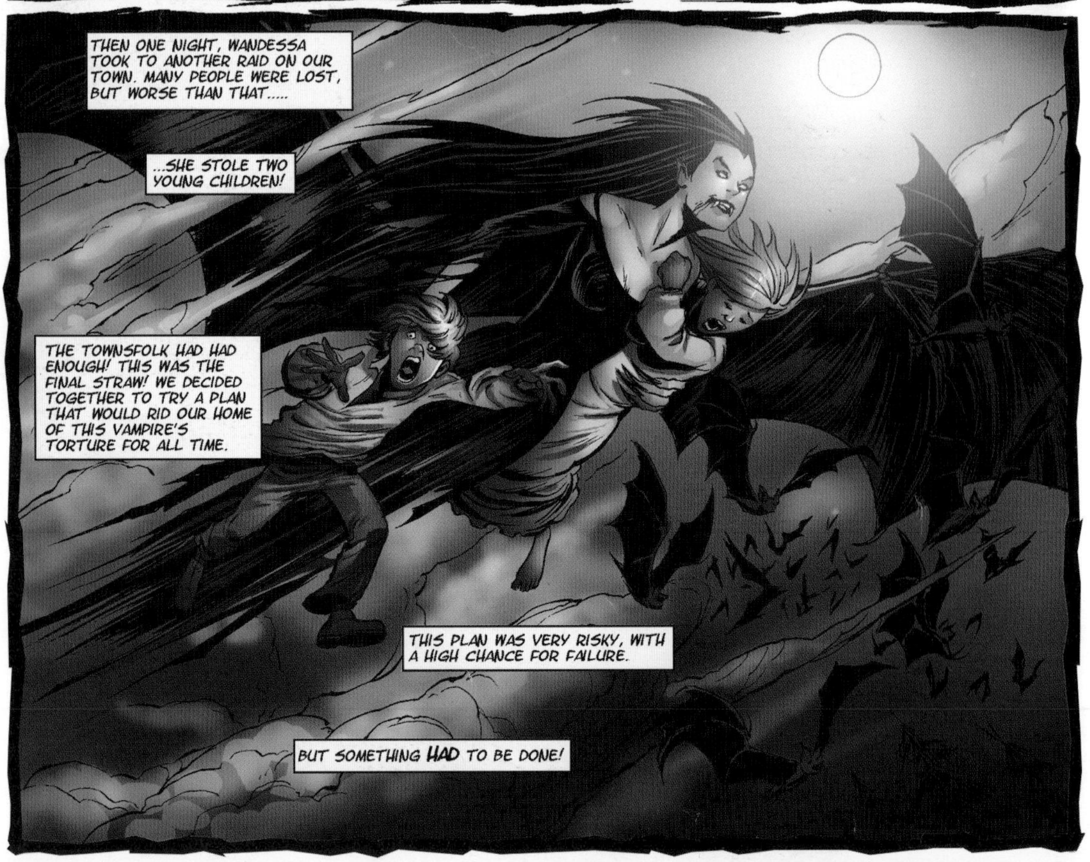
THEN ONE NIGHT, WANDESSA TOOK TO ANOTHER RAID ON OUR TOWN. MANY PEOPLE WERE LOST, BUT WORSE THAN THAT.....
...SHE STOLE TWO YOUNG CHILDREN!
THE TOWNSFOLK HAD HAD ENOUGH! THIS WAS THE FINAL STRAW! WE DECIDED TOGETHER TO TRY A PLAN THAT WOULD RID OUR HOME OF THIS VAMPIRE'S TORTURE FOR ALL TIME.
THIS PLAN WAS VERY RISKY, WITH A HIGH CHANCE FOR FAILURE.
BUT SOMETHING **HAD** TO BE DONE!

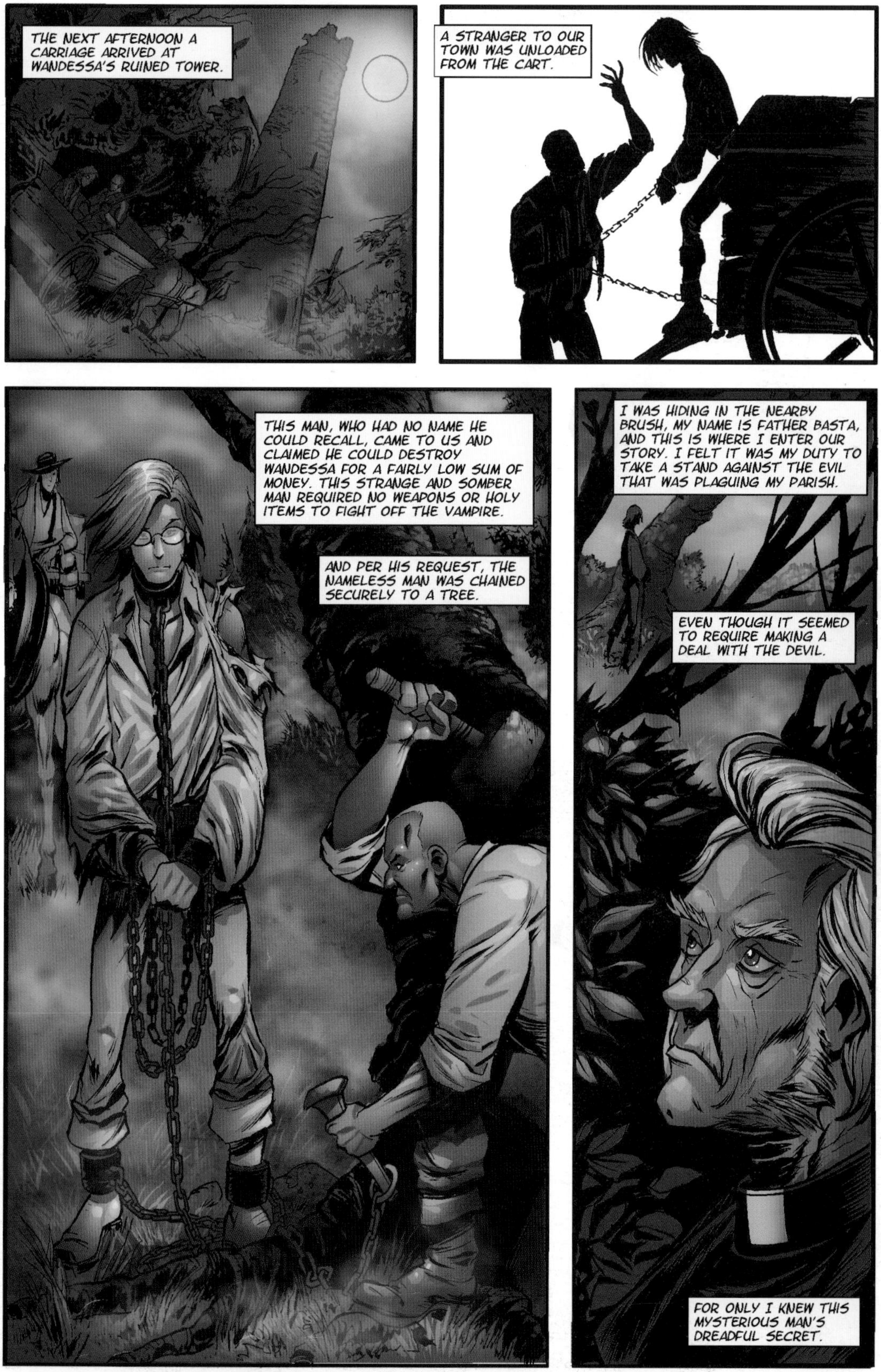
THE NEXT AFTERNOON A CARRIAGE ARRIVED AT WANDESSA'S RUINED TOWER.
A STRANGER TO OUR TOWN WAS UNLOADED FROM THE CART.
THIS MAN, WHO HAD NO NAME HE COULD RECALL, CAME TO US AND CLAIMED HE COULD DESTROY WANDESSA FOR A FAIRLY LOW SUM OF MONEY. THIS STRANGE AND SOMBER MAN REQUIRED NO WEAPONS OR HOLY ITEMS TO FIGHT OFF THE VAMPIRE.
AND PER HIS REQUEST, THE NAMELESS MAN WAS CHAINED SECURELY TO A TREE.
I WAS HIDING IN THE NEARBY BRUSH, MY NAME IS FATHER BASTA, AND THIS IS WHERE I ENTER OUR STORY. I FELT IT WAS MY DUTY TO TAKE A STAND AGAINST THE EVIL THAT WAS PLAGUING MY PARISH.
EVEN THOUGH IT SEEMED TO REQUIRE MAKING A DEAL WITH THE DEVIL.
FOR ONLY I KNEW THIS MYSTERIOUS MAN'S DREADFUL SECRET.

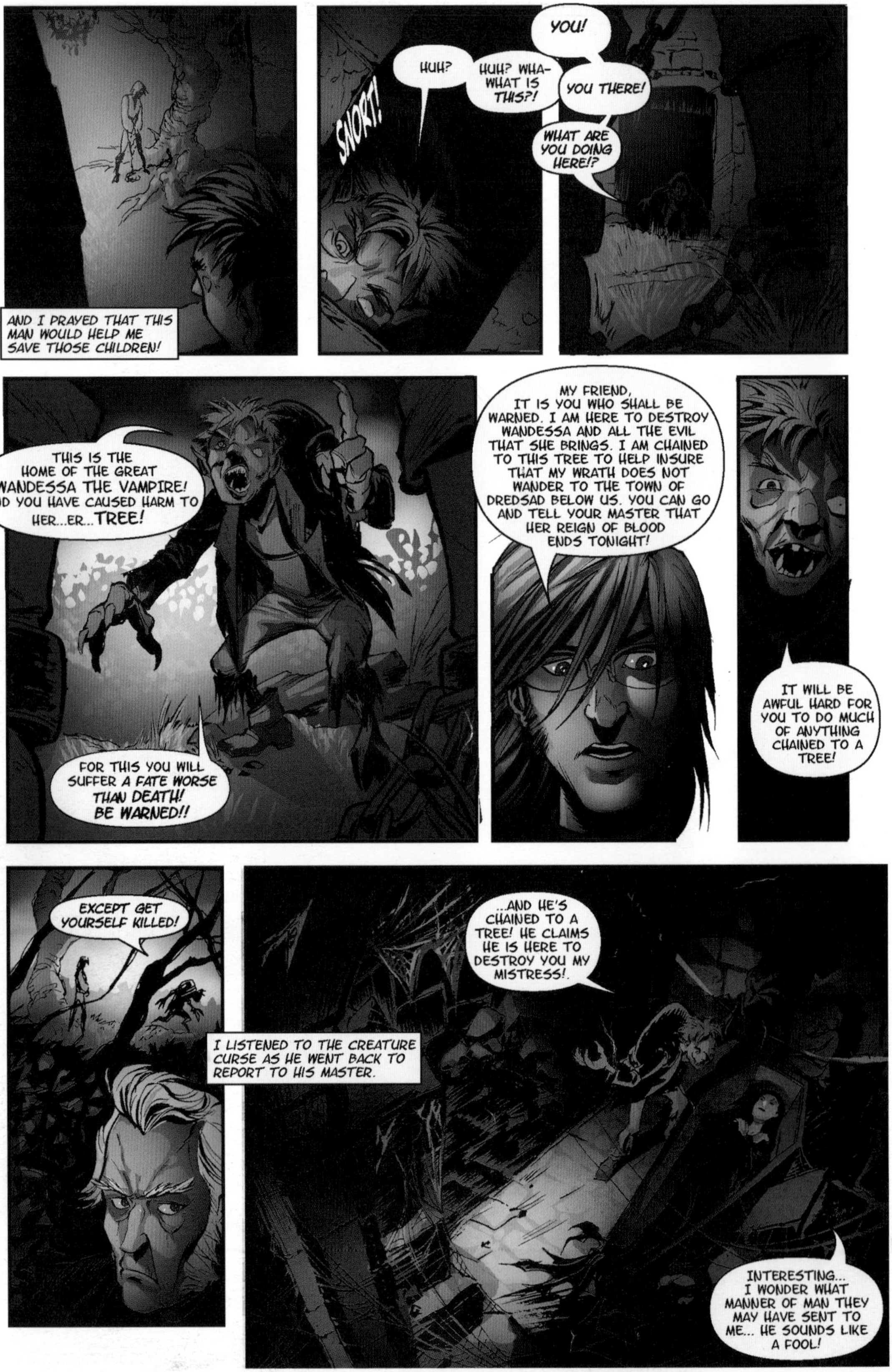
AND I PRAYED THAT THIS MAN WOULD HELP ME SAVE THOSE CHILDREN!
SNORT!
HUH?
HUH? WHA-WHAT IS THIS?!
YOU!
YOU THERE!
WHAT ARE YOU DOING HERE!?
THIS IS THE HOME OF THE GREAT WANDESSA THE VAMPIRE! AND YOU HAVE CAUSED HARM TO HER...ER...TREE!
FOR THIS YOU WILL SUFFER A FATE WORSE THAN DEATH! BE WARNED!!
MY FRIEND, IT IS YOU WHO SHALL BE WARNED. I AM HERE TO DESTROY WANDESSA AND ALL THE EVIL THAT SHE BRINGS. I AM CHAINED TO THIS TREE TO HELP INSURE THAT MY WRATH DOES NOT WANDER TO THE TOWN OF DREDSAD BELOW US. YOU CAN GO AND TELL YOUR MASTER THAT HER REIGN OF BLOOD ENDS TONIGHT!
IT WILL BE AWFUL HARD FOR YOU TO DO MUCH OF ANYTHING CHAINED TO A TREE!
EXCEPT GET YOURSELF KILLED!
I LISTENED TO THE CREATURE CURSE AS HE WENT BACK TO REPORT TO HIS MASTER.
...AND HE'S CHAINED TO A TREE! HE CLAIMS HE IS HERE TO DESTROY YOU MY MISTRESS!.
INTERESTING... I WONDER WHAT MANNER OF MAN THEY MAY HAVE SENT TO ME... HE SOUNDS LIKE A FOOL!

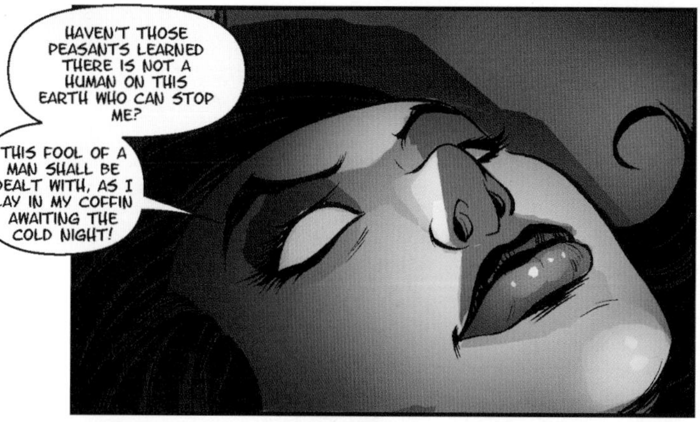
HAVEN'T THOSE PEASANTS LEARNED THERE IS NOT A HUMAN ON THIS EARTH WHO CAN STOP ME?
THIS FOOL OF A MAN SHALL BE DEALT WITH, AS I LAY IN MY COFFIN AWAITING THE COLD NIGHT!

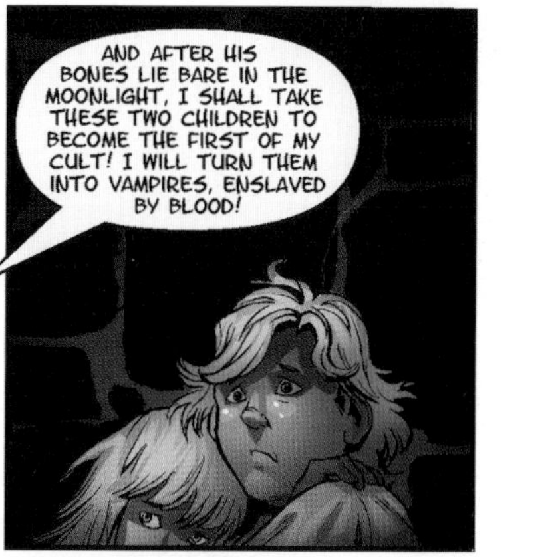
AND AFTER HIS BONES LIE BARE IN THE MOONLIGHT, I SHALL TAKE THESE TWO CHILDREN TO BECOME THE FIRST OF MY CULT! I WILL TURN THEM INTO VAMPIRES, ENSLAVED BY BLOOD!

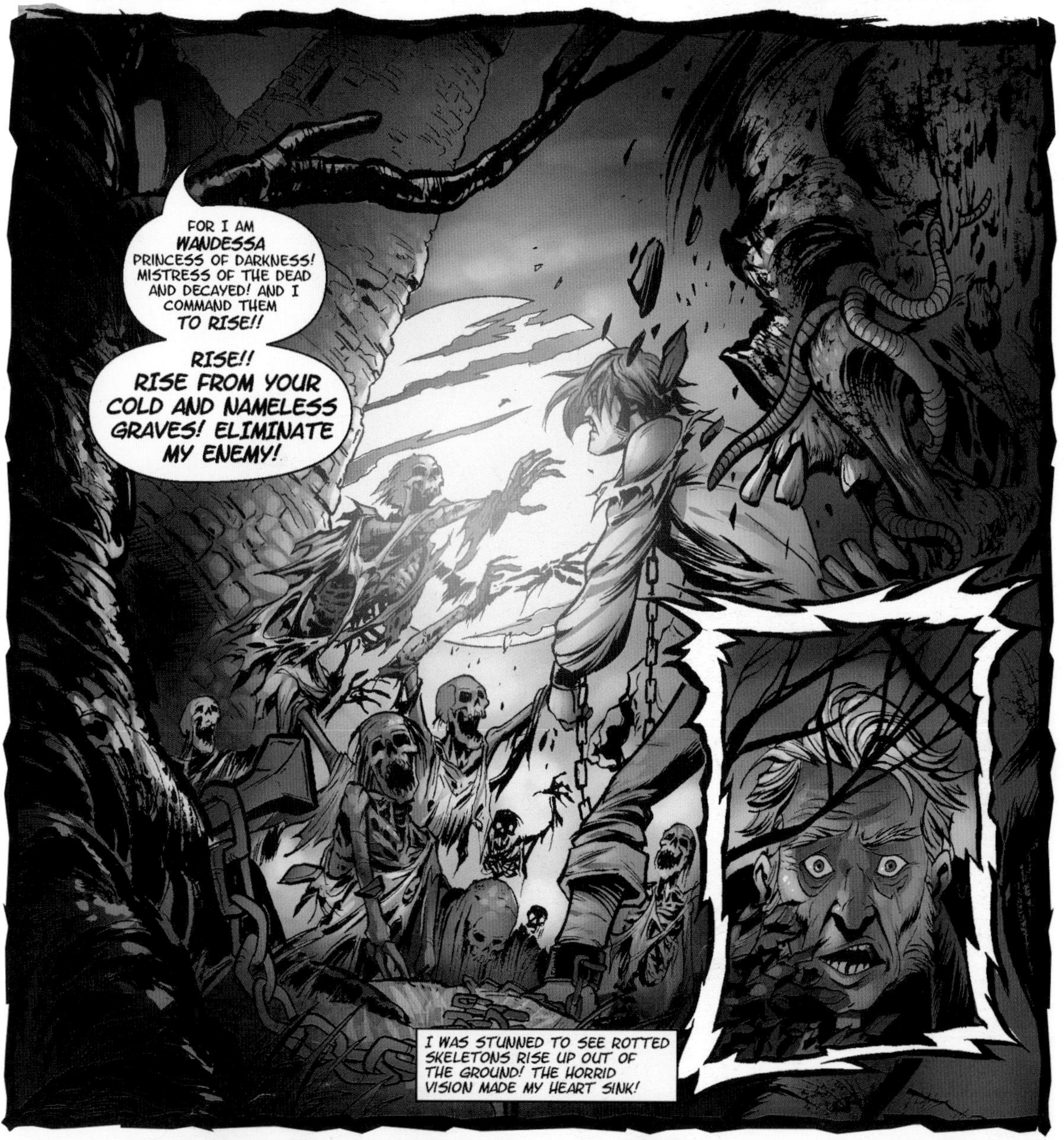
FOR I AM WANDESSA PRINCESS OF DARKNESS! MISTRESS OF THE DEAD AND DECAYED! AND I COMMAND THEM TO RISE!!
RISE!! RISE FROM YOUR COLD AND NAMELESS GRAVES! ELIMINATE MY ENEMY!
I WAS STUNNED TO SEE ROTTED SKELETONS RISE UP OUT OF THE GROUND! THE HORRID VISION MADE MY HEART SINK!

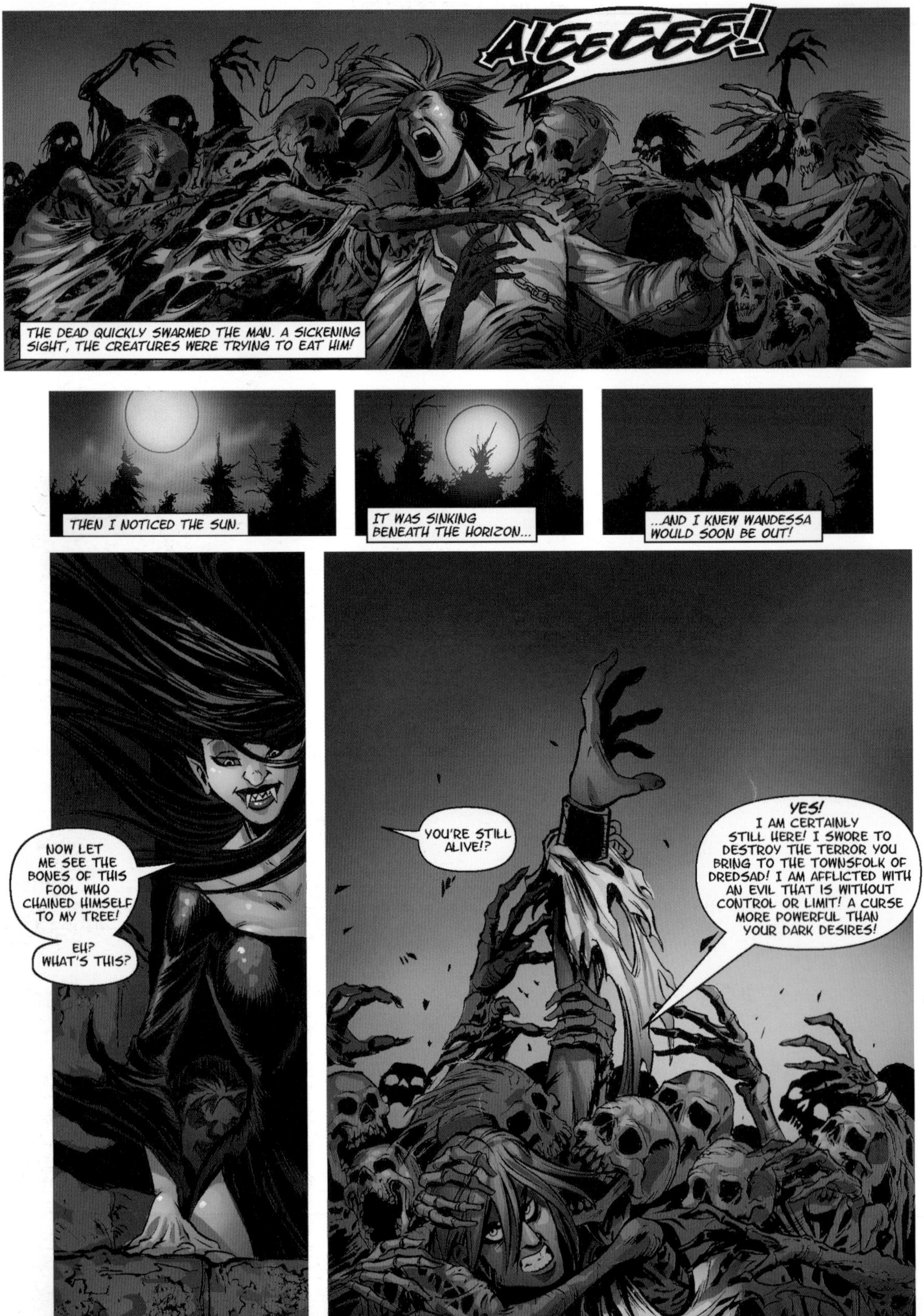
AIEEEEE!
THE DEAD QUICKLY SWARMED THE MAN. A SICKENING SIGHT, THE CREATURES WERE TRYING TO EAT HIM!
THEN I NOTICED THE SUN.
IT WAS SINKING BENEATH THE HORIZON...
...AND I KNEW WANDESSA WOULD SOON BE OUT!
NOW LET ME SEE THE BONES OF THIS FOOL WHO CHAINED HIMSELF TO MY TREE!
EH? WHAT'S THIS?
YOU'RE STILL ALIVE!?
YES! I AM CERTAINLY STILL HERE! I SWORE TO DESTROY THE TERROR YOU BRING TO THE TOWNSFOLK OF DREDSAD! I AM AFFLICTED WITH AN EVIL THAT IS WITHOUT CONTROL OR LIMIT! A CURSE MORE POWERFUL THAN YOUR DARK DESIRES!

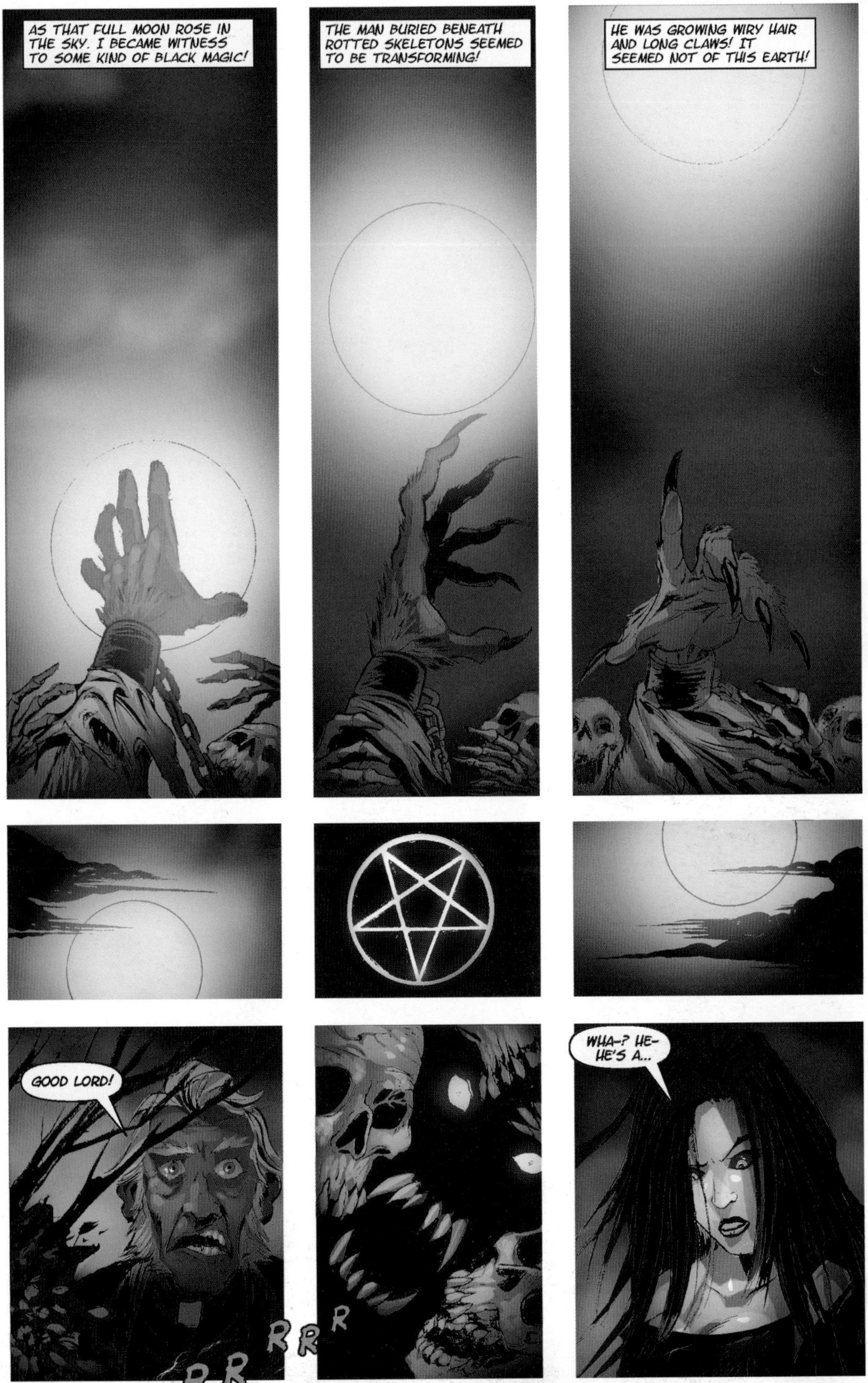
AS THAT FULL MOON ROSE IN THE SKY. I BECAME WITNESS TO SOME KIND OF BLACK MAGIC!
THE MAN BURIED BENEATH ROTTED SKELETONS SEEMED TO BE TRANSFORMING!
HE WAS GROWING WIRY HAIR AND LONG CLAWS! IT SEEMED NOT OF THIS EARTH!
GOOD LORD!
RRRRRR
WHA-? HE-HE'S A...

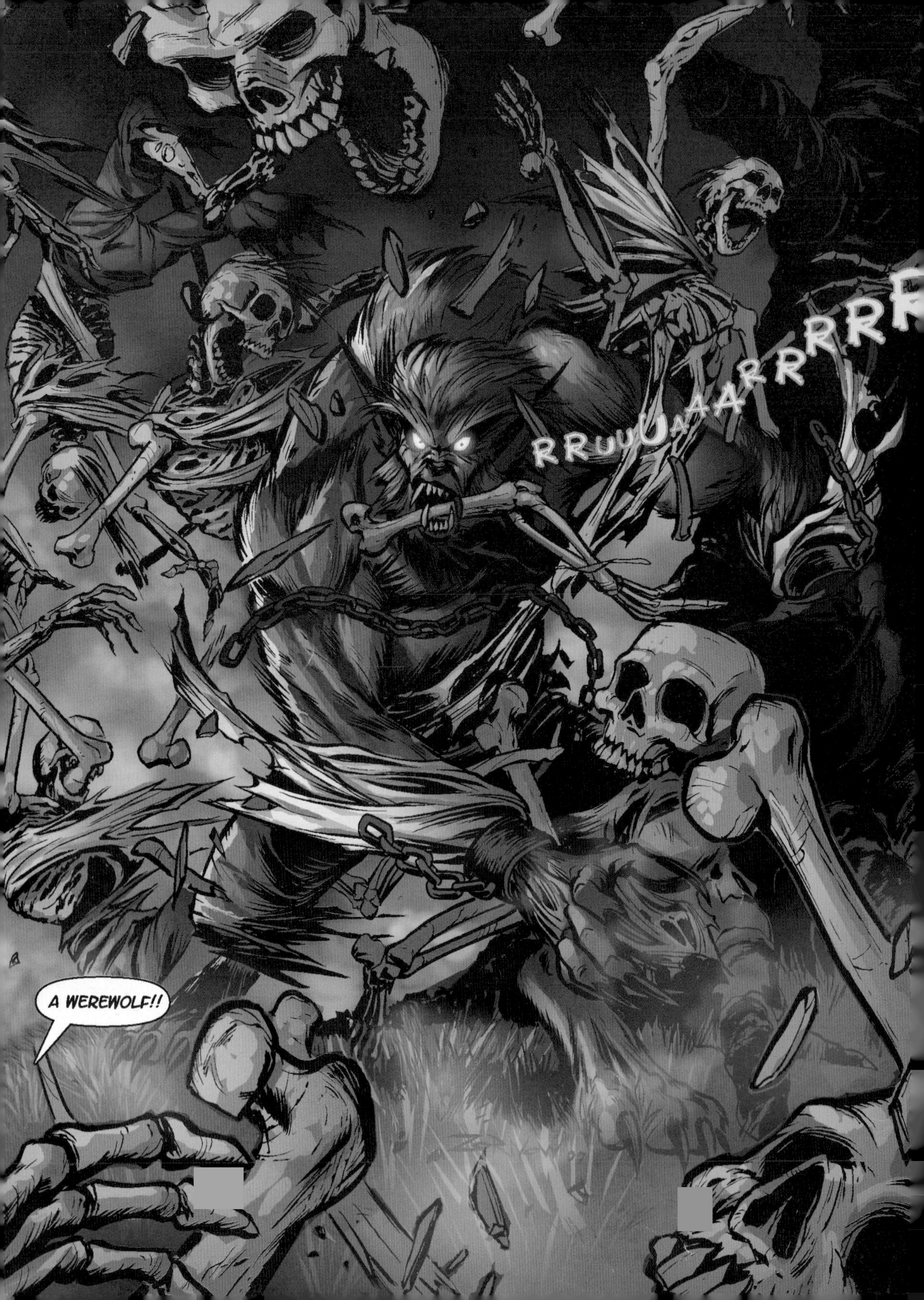
RRUUUAAARRRRRRR
A WEREWOLF!!

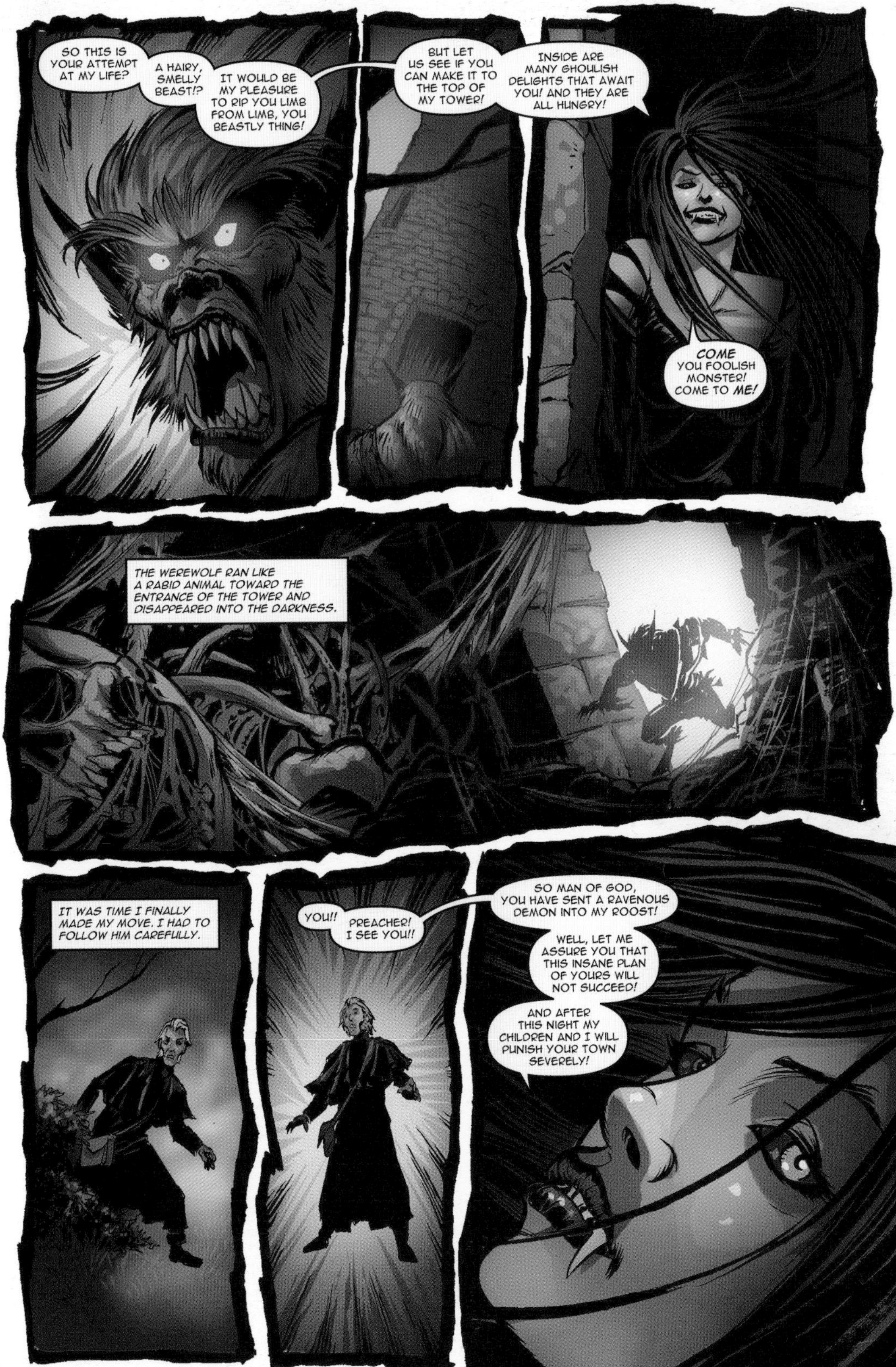
SO THIS IS YOUR ATTEMPT AT MY LIFE?
A HAIRY, SMELLY BEAST!?
IT WOULD BE MY PLEASURE TO RIP YOU LIMB FROM LIMB, YOU BEASTLY THING!
BUT LET US SEE IF YOU CAN MAKE IT TO THE TOP OF MY TOWER!
INSIDE ARE MANY GHOULISH DELIGHTS THAT AWAIT YOU! AND THEY ARE ALL HUNGRY!
COME YOU FOOLISH MONSTER! COME TO ME!
THE WEREWOLF RAN LIKE A RABID ANIMAL TOWARD THE ENTRANCE OF THE TOWER AND DISAPPEARED INTO THE DARKNESS.
IT WAS TIME I FINALLY MADE MY MOVE. I HAD TO FOLLOW HIM CAREFULLY.
YOU!!
PREACHER! I SEE YOU!!
SO MAN OF GOD, YOU HAVE SENT A RAVENOUS DEMON INTO MY ROOST!
WELL, LET ME ASSURE YOU THAT THIS INSANE PLAN OF YOURS WILL NOT SUCCEED!
AND AFTER THIS NIGHT MY CHILDREN AND I WILL PUNISH YOUR TOWN SEVERELY!

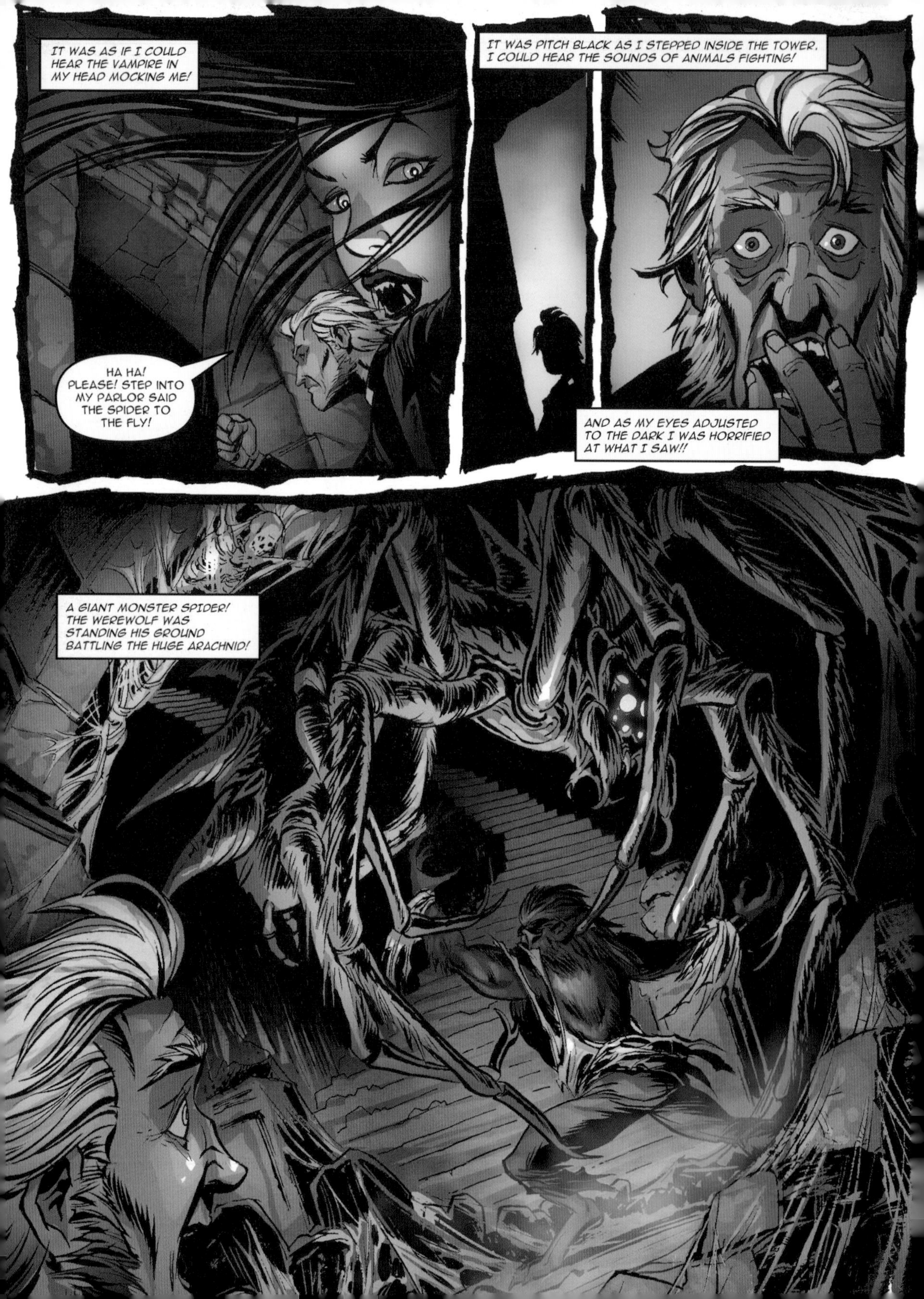
IT WAS AS IF I COULD HEAR THE VAMPIRE IN MY HEAD MOCKING ME!
HA HA! PLEASE! STEP INTO MY PARLOR SAID THE SPIDER TO THE FLY!
IT WAS PITCH BLACK AS I STEPPED INSIDE THE TOWER. I COULD HEAR THE SOUNDS OF ANIMALS FIGHTING!
AND AS MY EYES ADJUSTED TO THE DARK I WAS HORRIFIED AT WHAT I SAW!!
A GIANT MONSTER SPIDER! THE WEREWOLF WAS STANDING HIS GROUND BATTLING THE HUGE ARACHNID!

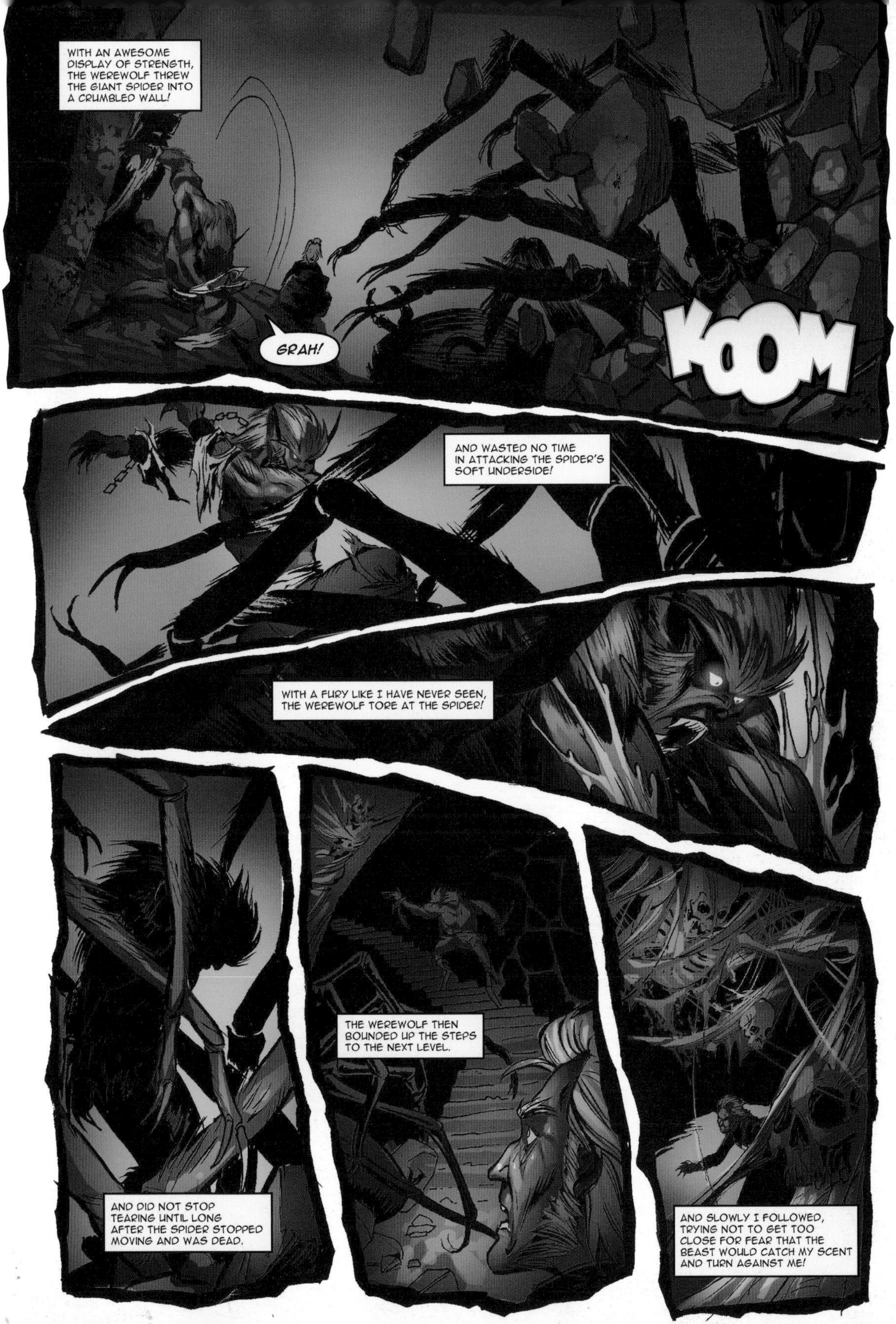
WITH AN AWESOME DISPLAY OF STRENGTH, THE WEREWOLF THREW THE GIANT SPIDER INTO A CRUMBLED WALL!
GRAH!
KOOM
AND WASTED NO TIME IN ATTACKING THE SPIDER'S SOFT UNDERSIDE!
WITH A FURY LIKE I HAVE NEVER SEEN, THE WEREWOLF TORE AT THE SPIDER!
AND DID NOT STOP TEARING UNTIL LONG AFTER THE SPIDER STOPPED MOVING AND WAS DEAD.
THE WEREWOLF THEN BOUNDED UP THE STEPS TO THE NEXT LEVEL.
AND SLOWLY I FOLLOWED, TRYING NOT TO GET TOO CLOSE FOR FEAR THAT THE BEAST WOULD CATCH MY SCENT AND TURN AGAINST ME!

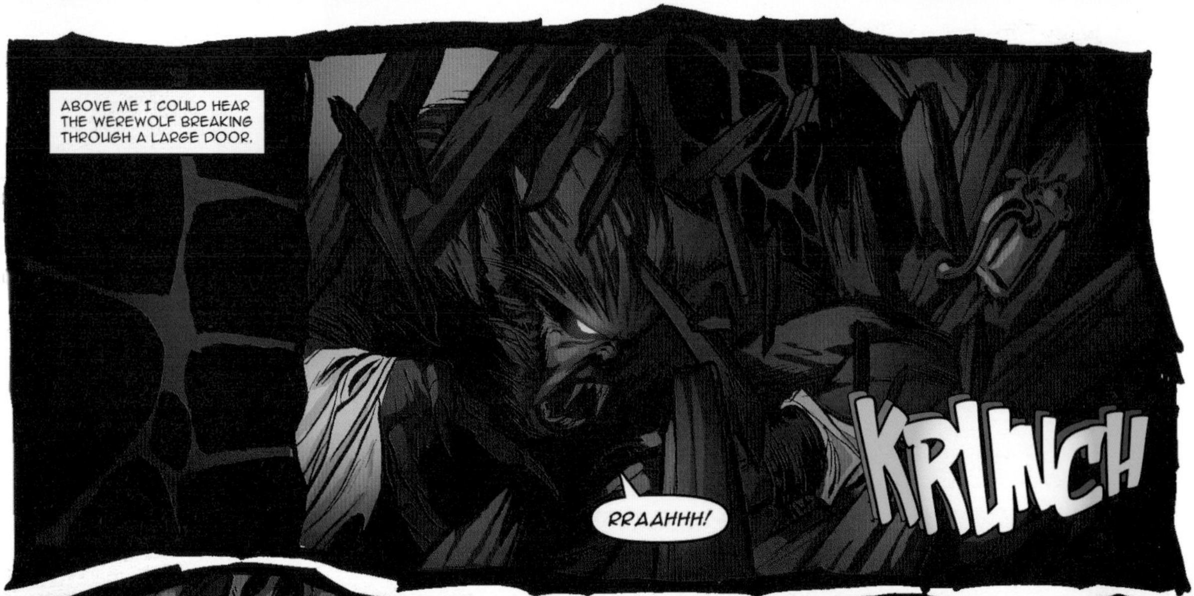
ABOVE ME I COULD HEAR THE WEREWOLF BREAKING THROUGH A LARGE DOOR.
KRUNCH
RRAAHHH!

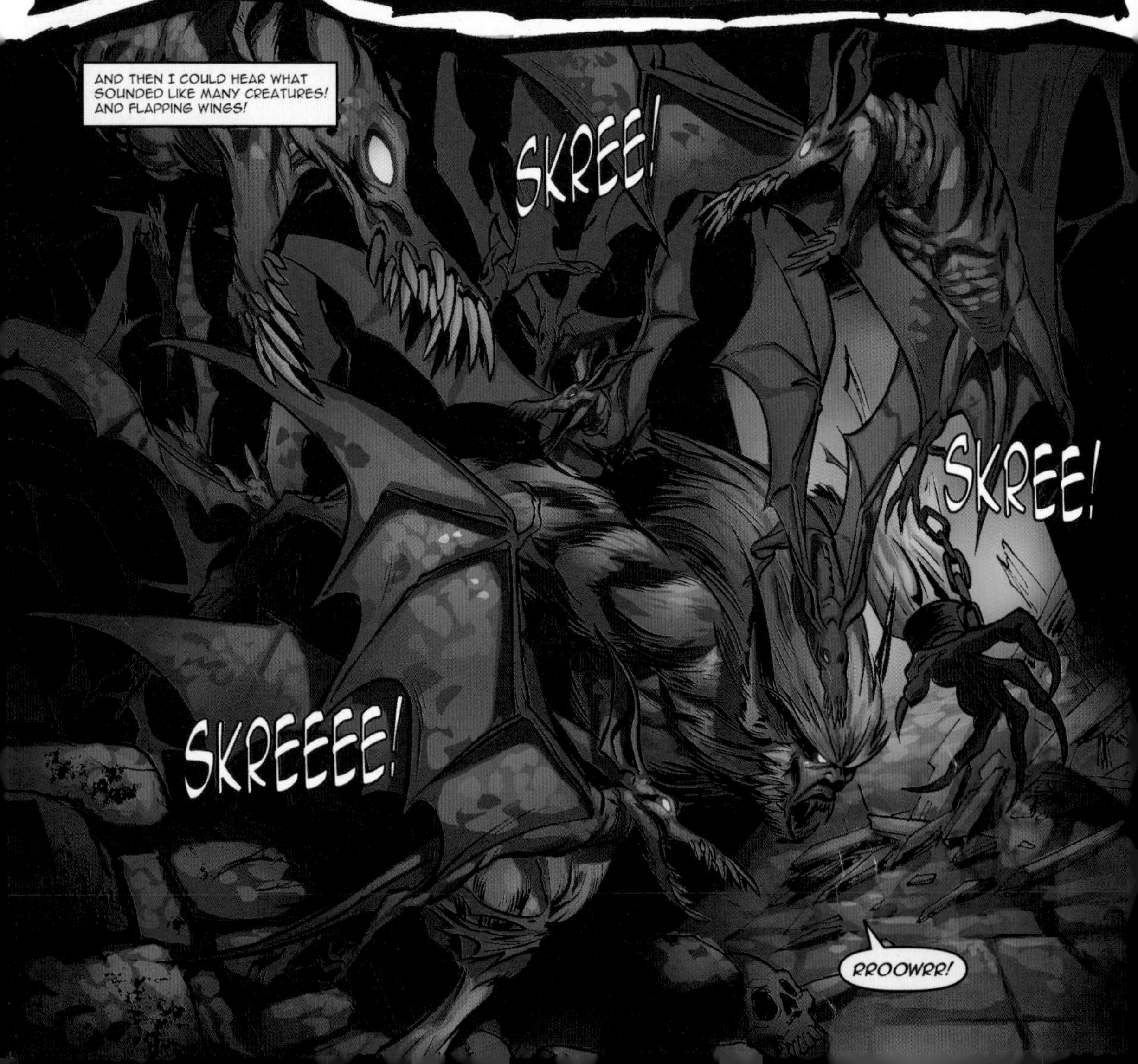
AND THEN I COULD HEAR WHAT SOUNDED LIKE MANY CREATURES! AND FLAPPING WINGS!
SKREE!
SKREE!
SKREEEE!
RROOWRR!

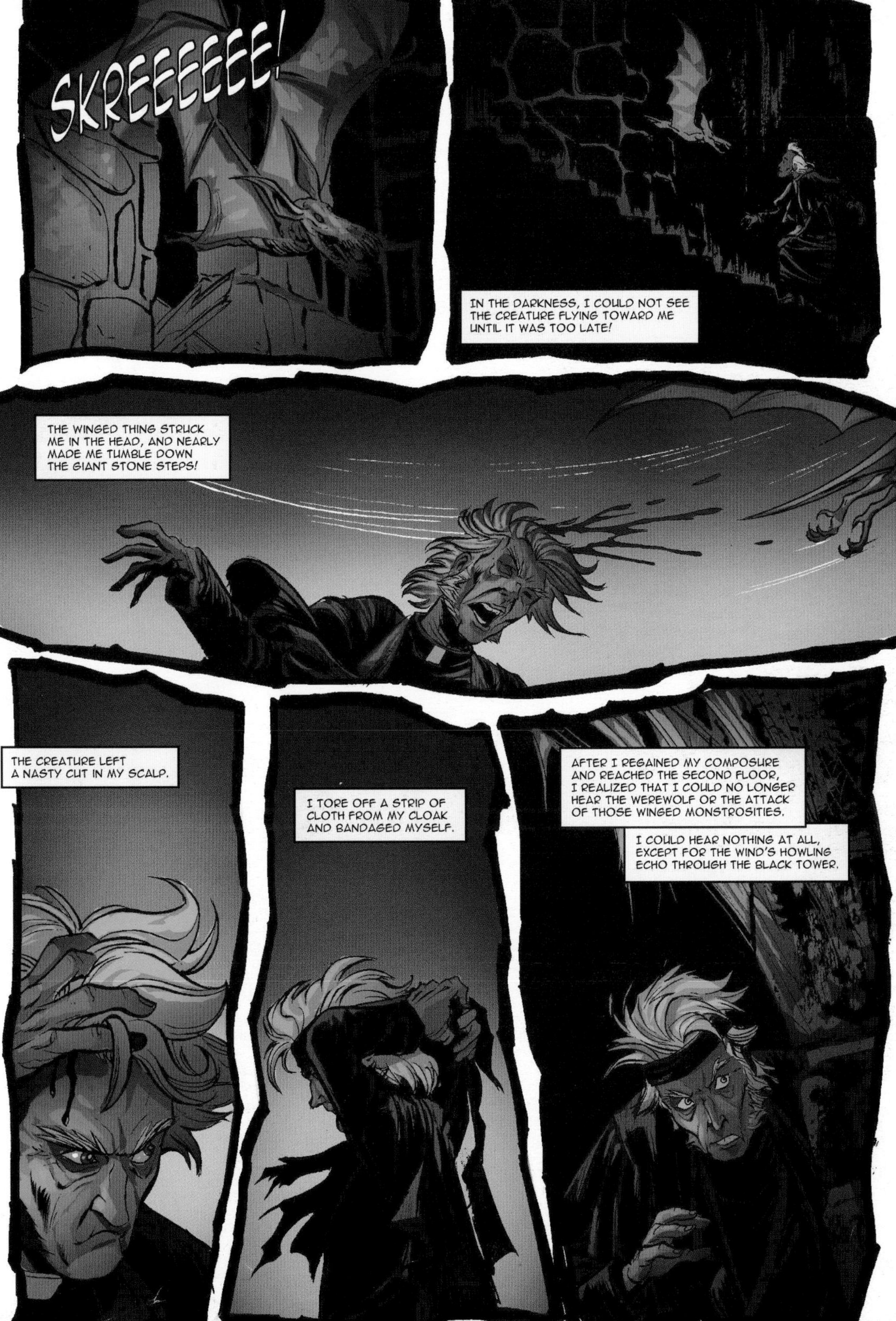
SKREEEEEEE!
IN THE DARKNESS, I COULD NOT SEE THE CREATURE FLYING TOWARD ME UNTIL IT WAS TOO LATE!
THE WINGED THING STRUCK ME IN THE HEAD, AND NEARLY MADE ME TUMBLE DOWN THE GIANT STONE STEPS!
THE CREATURE LEFT A NASTY CUT IN MY SCALP.
I TORE OFF A STRIP OF CLOTH FROM MY CLOAK AND BANDAGED MYSELF.
AFTER I REGAINED MY COMPOSURE AND REACHED THE SECOND FLOOR, I REALIZED THAT I COULD NO LONGER HEAR THE WEREWOLF OR THE ATTACK OF THOSE WINGED MONSTROSITIES.
I COULD HEAR NOTHING AT ALL, EXCEPT FOR THE WIND'S HOWLING ECHO THROUGH THE BLACK TOWER.

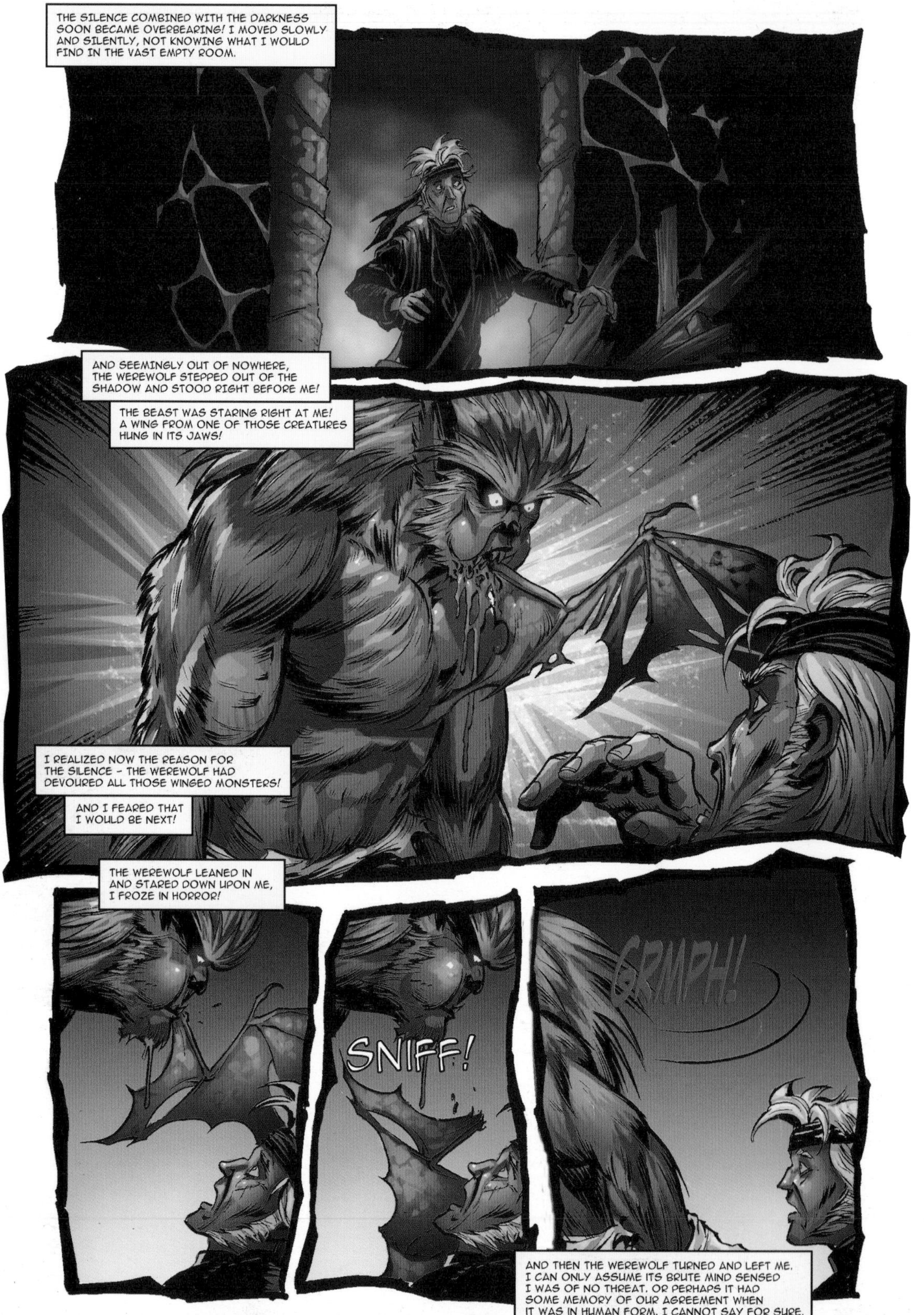
THE SILENCE COMBINED WITH THE DARKNESS SOON BECAME OVERBEARING! I MOVED SLOWLY AND SILENTLY, NOT KNOWING WHAT I WOULD FIND IN THE VAST EMPTY ROOM.
AND SEEMINGLY OUT OF NOWHERE, THE WEREWOLF STEPPED OUT OF THE SHADOW AND STOOD RIGHT BEFORE ME!
THE BEAST WAS STARING RIGHT AT ME! A WING FROM ONE OF THOSE CREATURES HUNG IN ITS JAWS!
I REALIZED NOW THE REASON FOR THE SILENCE - THE WEREWOLF HAD DEVOURED ALL THOSE WINGED MONSTERS!
AND I FEARED THAT I WOULD BE NEXT!
THE WEREWOLF LEANED IN AND STARED DOWN UPON ME, I FROZE IN HORROR!
SNIFF!
GRMPH!
AND THEN THE WEREWOLF TURNED AND LEFT ME. I CAN ONLY ASSUME ITS BRUTE MIND SENSED I WAS OF NO THREAT. OR PERHAPS IT HAD SOME MEMORY OF OUR AGREEMENT WHEN IT WAS IN HUMAN FORM. I CANNOT SAY FOR SURE.

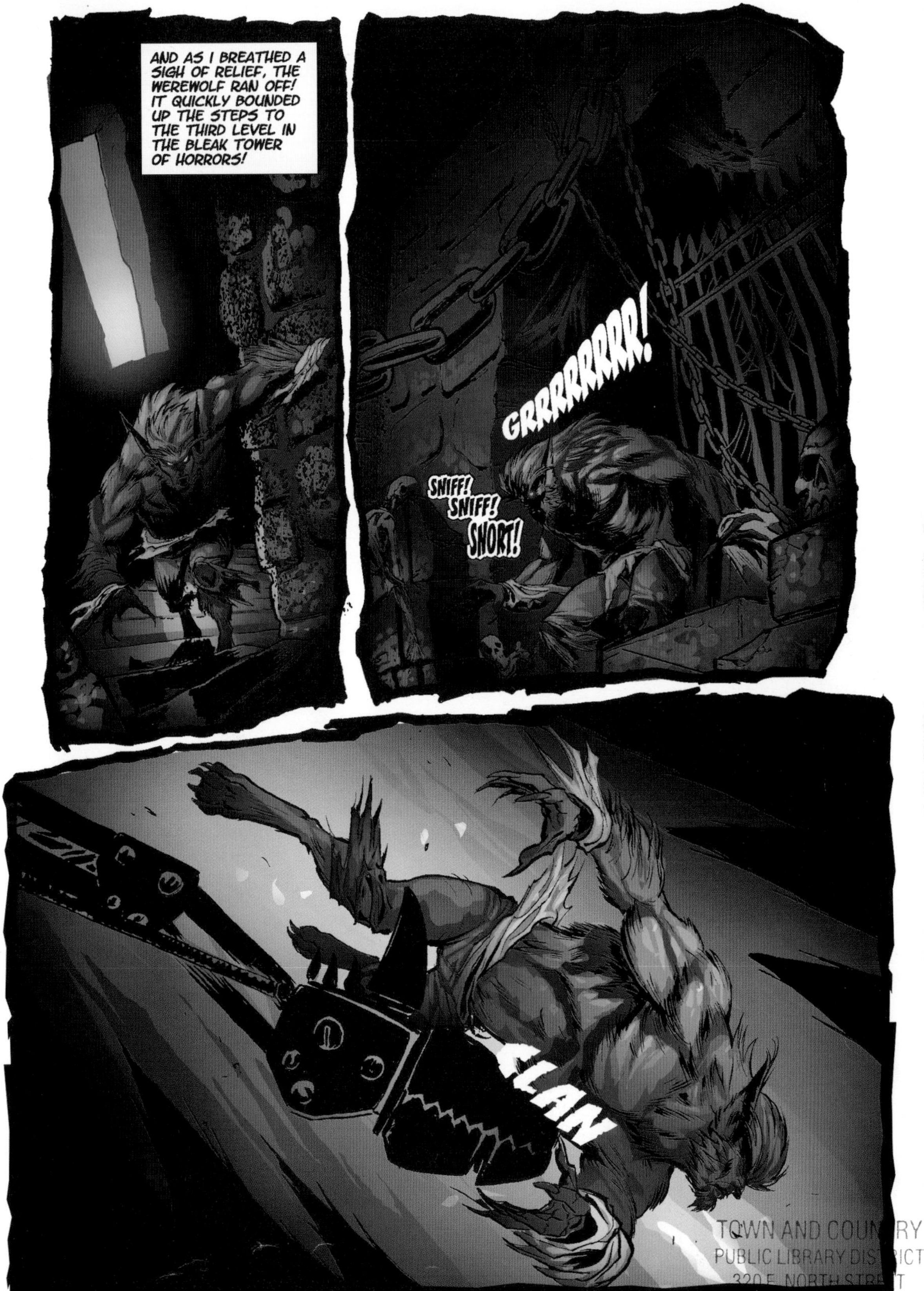
AND AS I BREATHED A SIGH OF RELIEF, THE WEREWOLF RAN OFF! IT QUICKLY BOUNDED UP THE STEPS TO THE THIRD LEVEL IN THE BLEAK TOWER OF HORRORS!
GRRRRRRRR!
SNIFF!
SNIFF!
SNORT!
CLAN

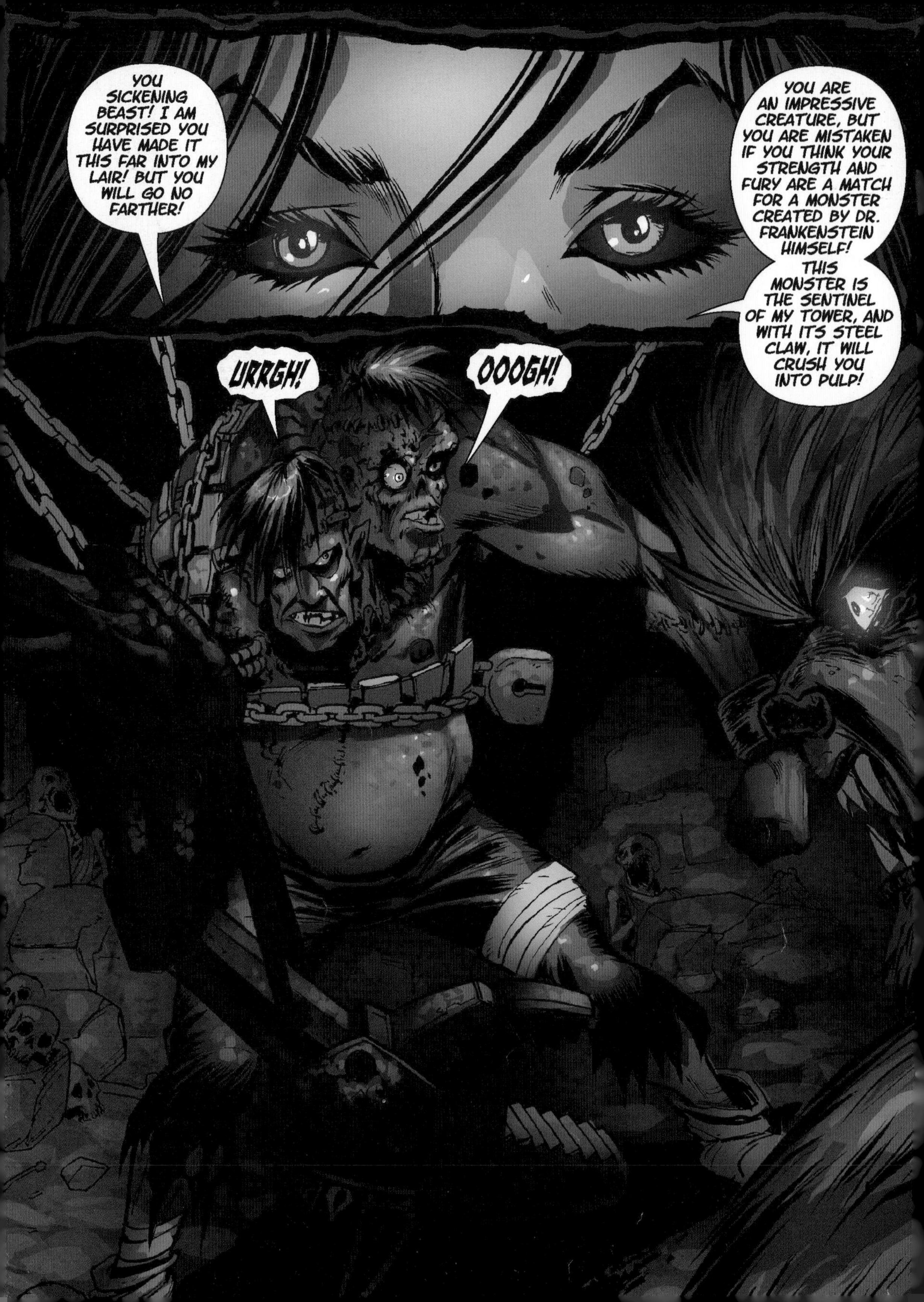
YOU SICKENING BEAST! I AM SURPRISED YOU HAVE MADE IT THIS FAR INTO MY LAIR! BUT YOU WILL GO NO FARTHER!
YOU ARE AN IMPRESSIVE CREATURE, BUT YOU ARE MISTAKEN IF YOU THINK YOUR STRENGTH AND FURY ARE A MATCH FOR A MONSTER CREATED BY DR. FRANKENSTEIN HIMSELF!
THIS MONSTER IS THE SENTINEL OF MY TOWER, AND WITH ITS STEEL CLAW, IT WILL CRUSH YOU INTO PULP!
URRGH!
OOOGH!

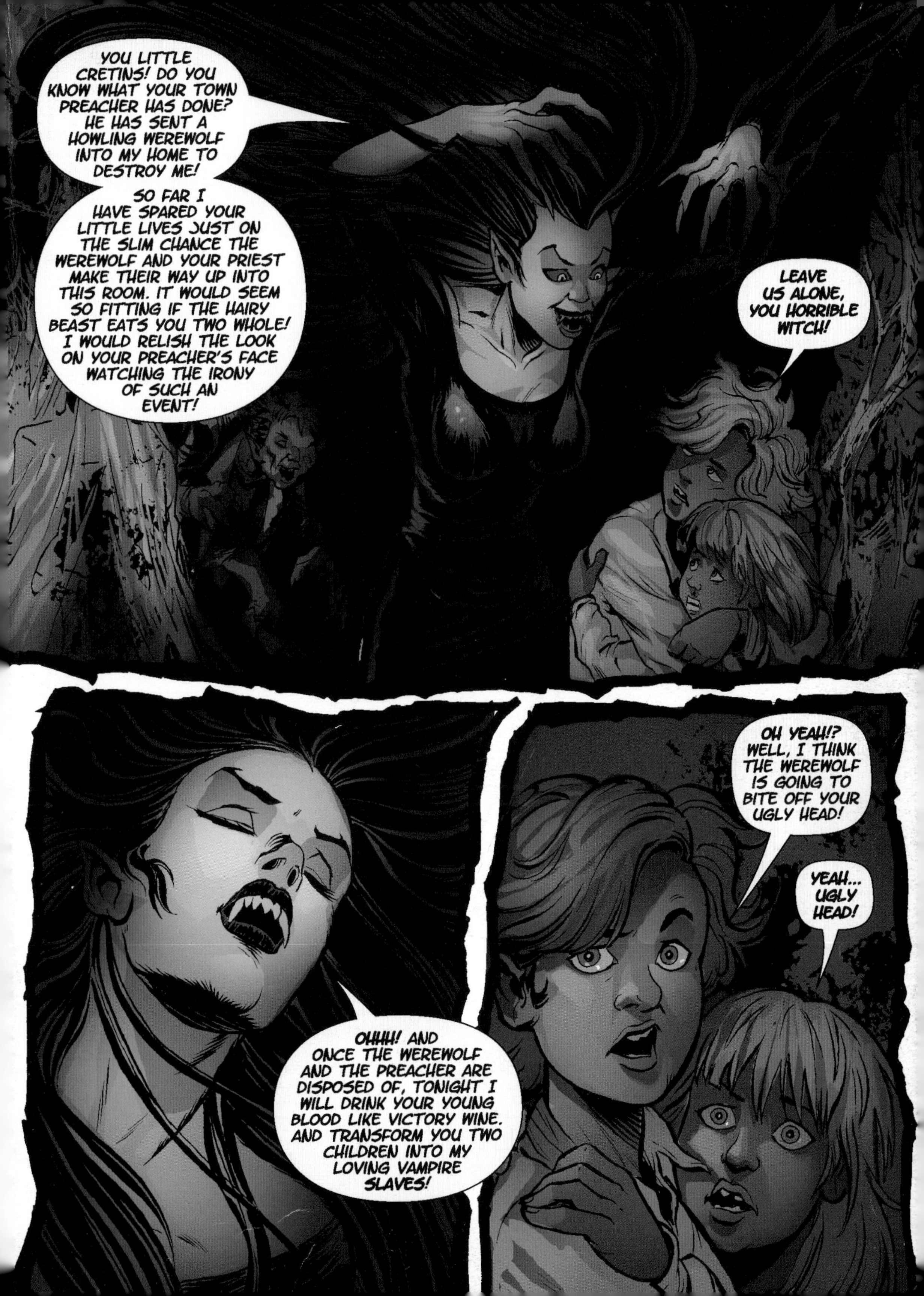
YOU LITTLE CRETINS! DO YOU KNOW WHAT YOUR TOWN PREACHER HAS DONE? HE HAS SENT A HOWLING WEREWOLF INTO MY HOME TO DESTROY ME!
SO FAR I HAVE SPARED YOUR LITTLE LIVES JUST ON THE SLIM CHANCE THE WEREWOLF AND YOUR PRIEST MAKE THEIR WAY UP INTO THIS ROOM. IT WOULD SEEM SO FITTING IF THE HAIRY BEAST EATS YOU TWO WHOLE! I WOULD RELISH THE LOOK ON YOUR PREACHER'S FACE WATCHING THE IRONY OF SUCH AN EVENT!
LEAVE US ALONE, YOU HORRIBLE WITCH!
OHHH! AND ONCE THE WEREWOLF AND THE PREACHER ARE DISPOSED OF, TONIGHT I WILL DRINK YOUR YOUNG BLOOD LIKE VICTORY WINE. AND TRANSFORM YOU TWO CHILDREN INTO MY LOVING VAMPIRE SLAVES!
OH YEAH!? WELL, I THINK THE WEREWOLF IS GOING TO BITE OFF YOUR UGLY HEAD!
YEAH... UGLY HEAD!

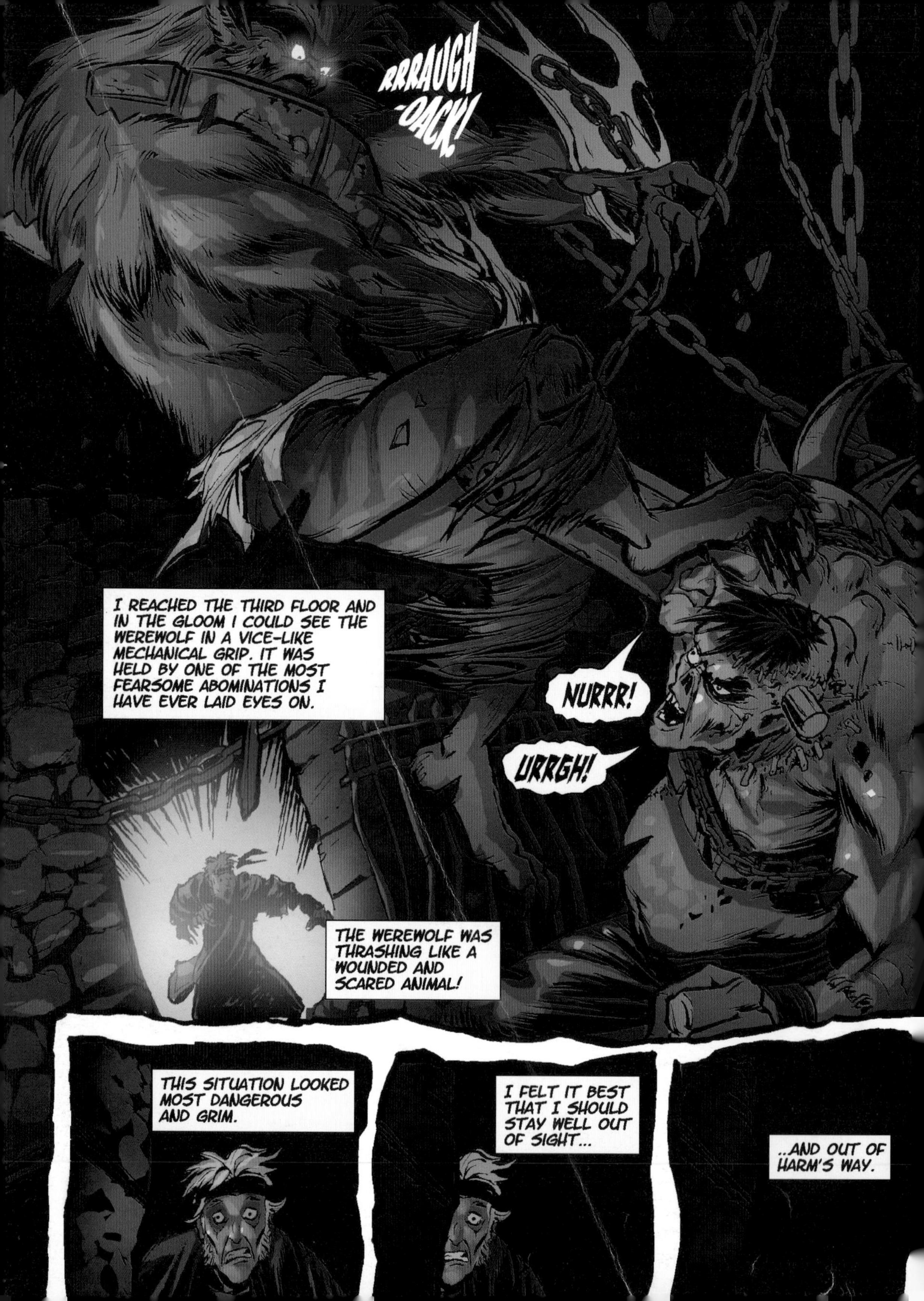
RRRAUGH -OACK!
I REACHED THE THIRD FLOOR AND IN THE GLOOM I COULD SEE THE WEREWOLF IN A VICE-LIKE MECHANICAL GRIP. IT WAS HELD BY ONE OF THE MOST FEARSOME ABOMINATIONS I HAVE EVER LAID EYES ON.
NURRR!
URRGH!
THE WEREWOLF WAS THRASHING LIKE A WOUNDED AND SCARED ANIMAL!
THIS SITUATION LOOKED MOST DANGEROUS AND GRIM.
I FELT IT BEST THAT I SHOULD STAY WELL OUT OF SIGHT...
...AND OUT OF HARM'S WAY.

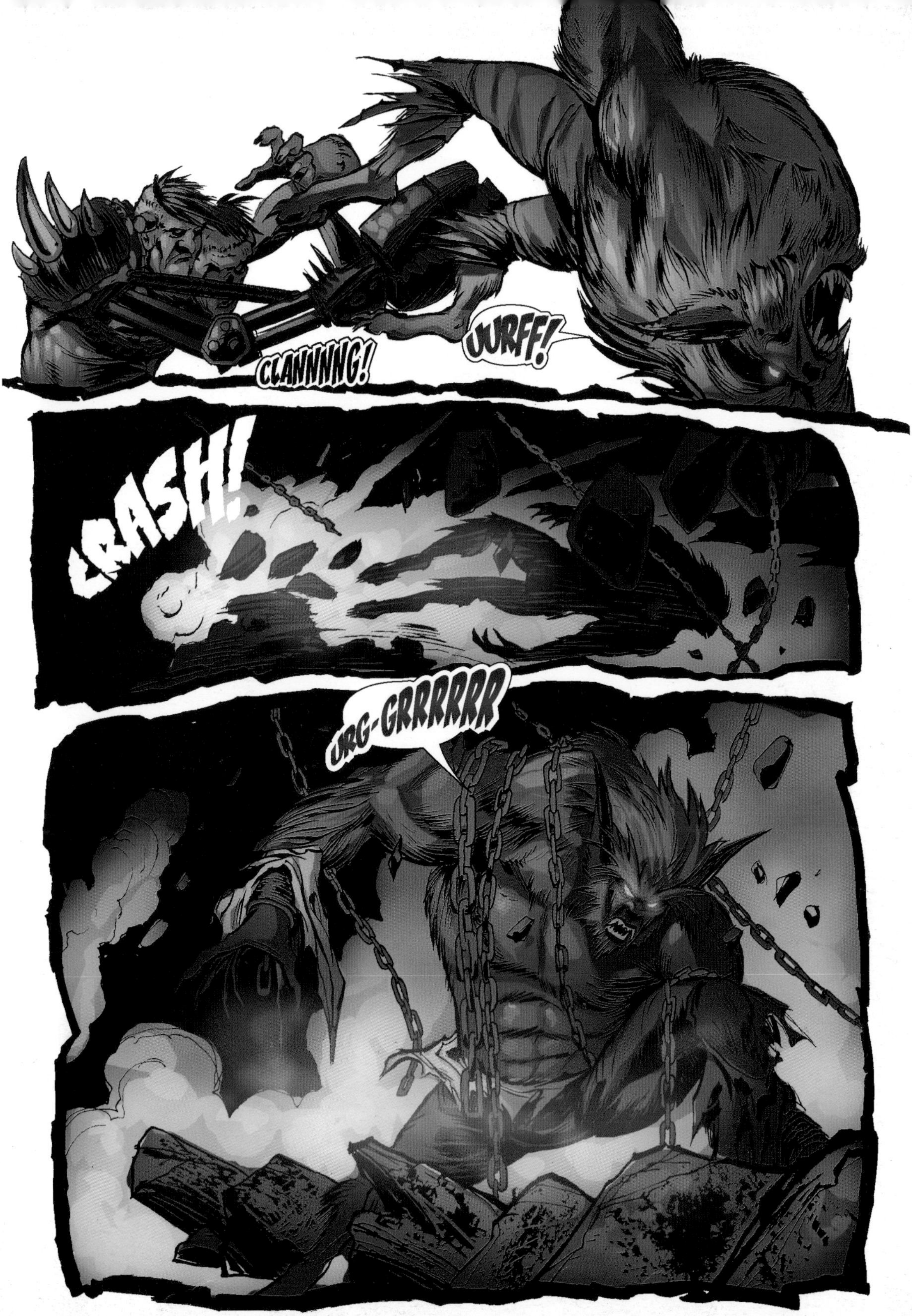
CLANNNNG!
UURFF!
CRASH!
URG-GRRRRRR

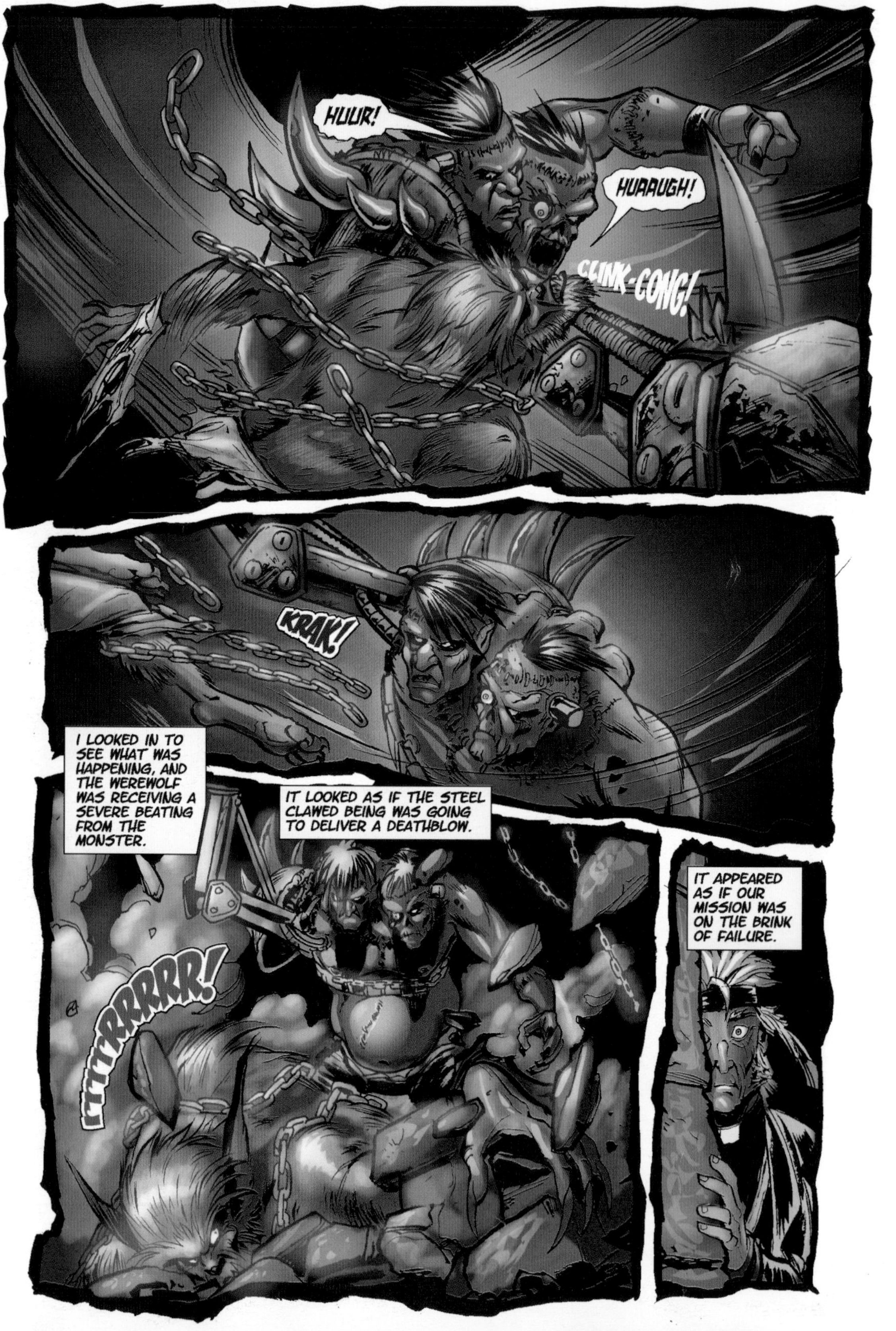
HUUR!
HURAUGH!
CLINK-CONG!
KRAK!
I LOOKED IN TO SEE WHAT WAS HAPPENING, AND THE WEREWOLF WAS RECEIVING A SEVERE BEATING FROM THE MONSTER.
IT LOOKED AS IF THE STEEL CLAWED BEING WAS GOING TO DELIVER A DEATHBLOW.
IT APPEARED AS IF OUR MISSION WAS ON THE BRINK OF FAILURE.
GRRRRR!

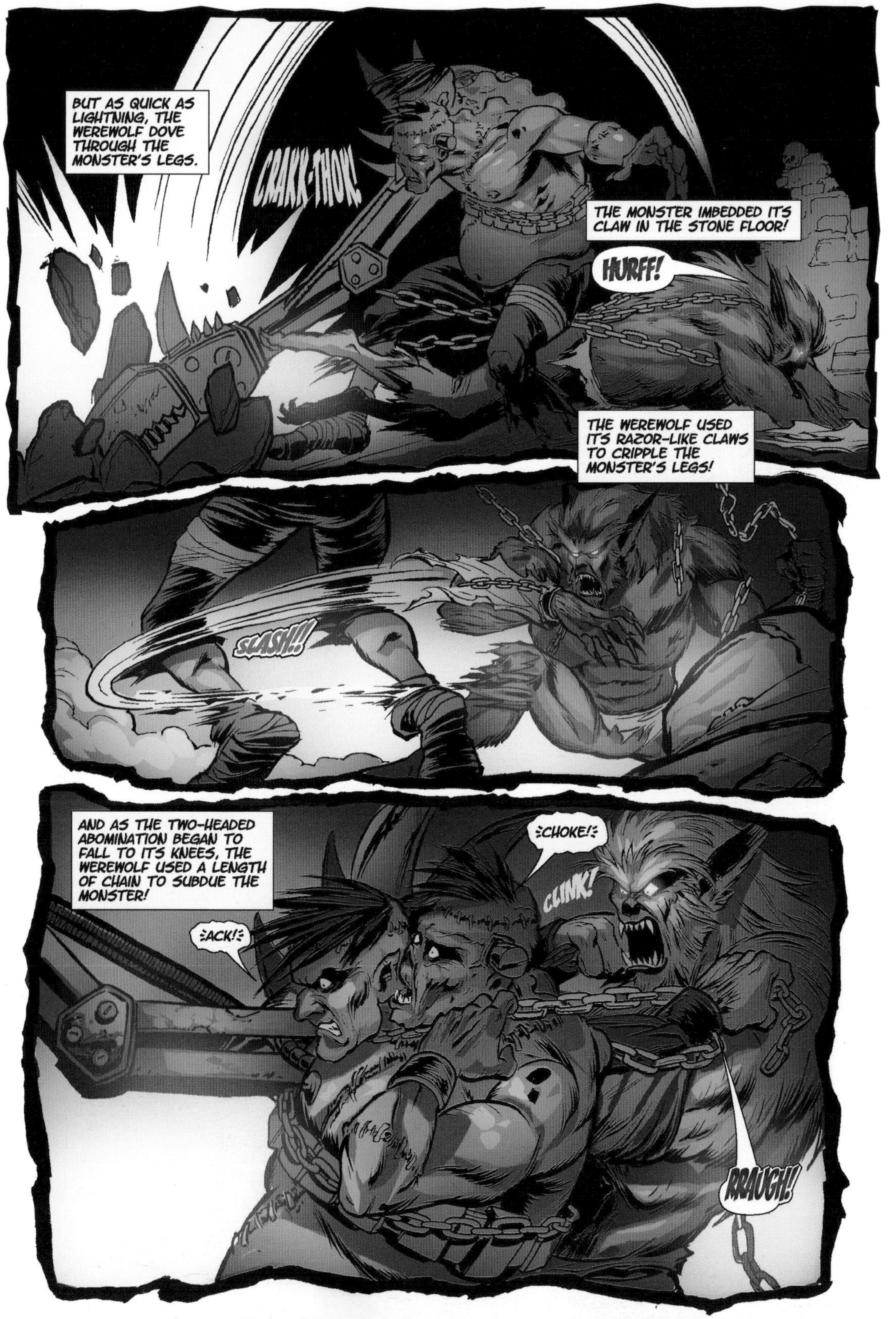
BUT AS QUICK AS LIGHTNING, THE WEREWOLF DOVE THROUGH THE MONSTER'S LEGS.
CRAKK-THOK!
THE MONSTER IMBEDDED ITS CLAW IN THE STONE FLOOR!
HURFF!
THE WEREWOLF USED ITS RAZOR-LIKE CLAWS TO CRIPPLE THE MONSTER'S LEGS!
SLASH!!
AND AS THE TWO-HEADED ABOMINATION BEGAN TO FALL TO ITS KNEES, THE WEREWOLF USED A LENGTH OF CHAIN TO SUBDUE THE MONSTER!
CHOKE!
CLINK!
ACK!
RRAUGH!

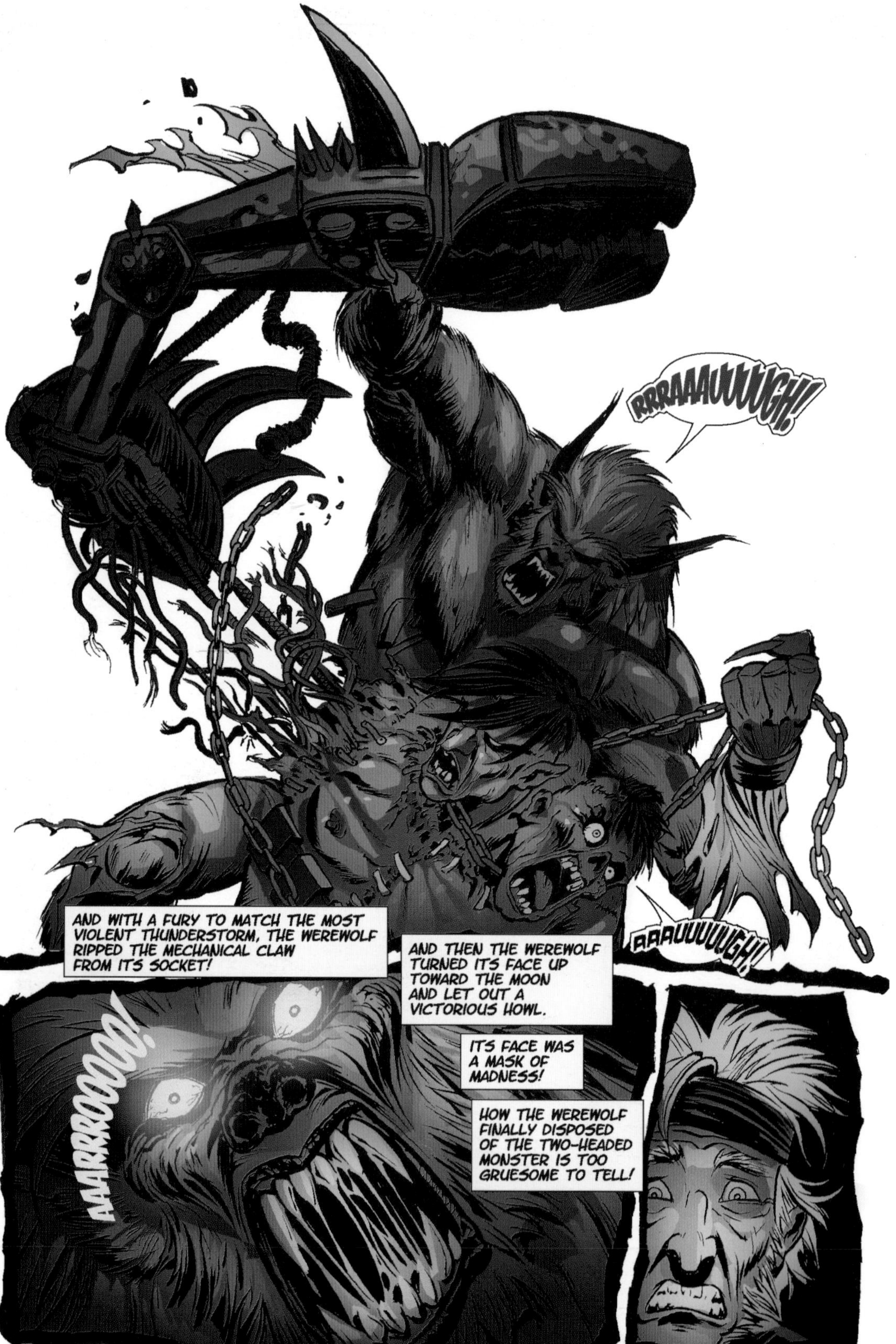
RRRAAAUUUUGH!
AND WITH A FURY TO MATCH THE MOST VIOLENT THUNDERSTORM, THE WEREWOLF RIPPED THE MECHANICAL CLAW FROM ITS SOCKET!
AAAUUUUUGH!
AND THEN THE WEREWOLF TURNED ITS FACE UP TOWARD THE MOON AND LET OUT A VICTORIOUS HOWL.
AAAARRROOOO!
ITS FACE WAS A MASK OF MADNESS!
HOW THE WEREWOLF FINALLY DISPOSED OF THE TWO-HEADED MONSTER IS TOO GRUESOME TO TELL!

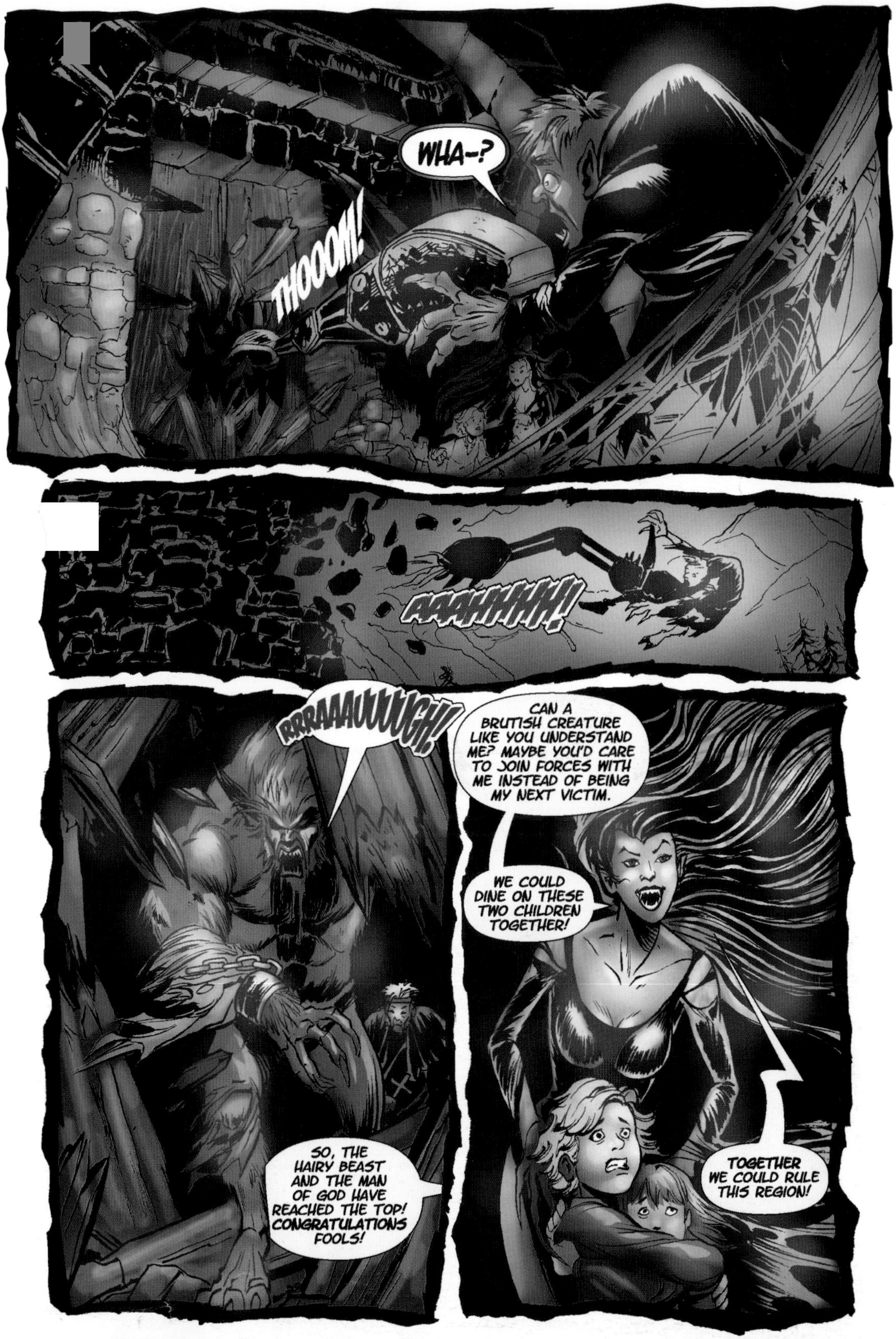
WHA--?
THOOOM!
RRRAAAUUUUGH!
SO, THE HAIRY BEAST AND THE MAN OF GOD HAVE REACHED THE TOP! CONGRATULATIONS FOOLS!
CAN A BRUTISH CREATURE LIKE YOU UNDERSTAND ME? MAYBE YOU'D CARE TO JOIN FORCES WITH ME INSTEAD OF BEING MY NEXT VICTIM.
WE COULD DINE ON THESE TWO CHILDREN TOGETHER!
TOGETHER WE COULD RULE THIS REGION!

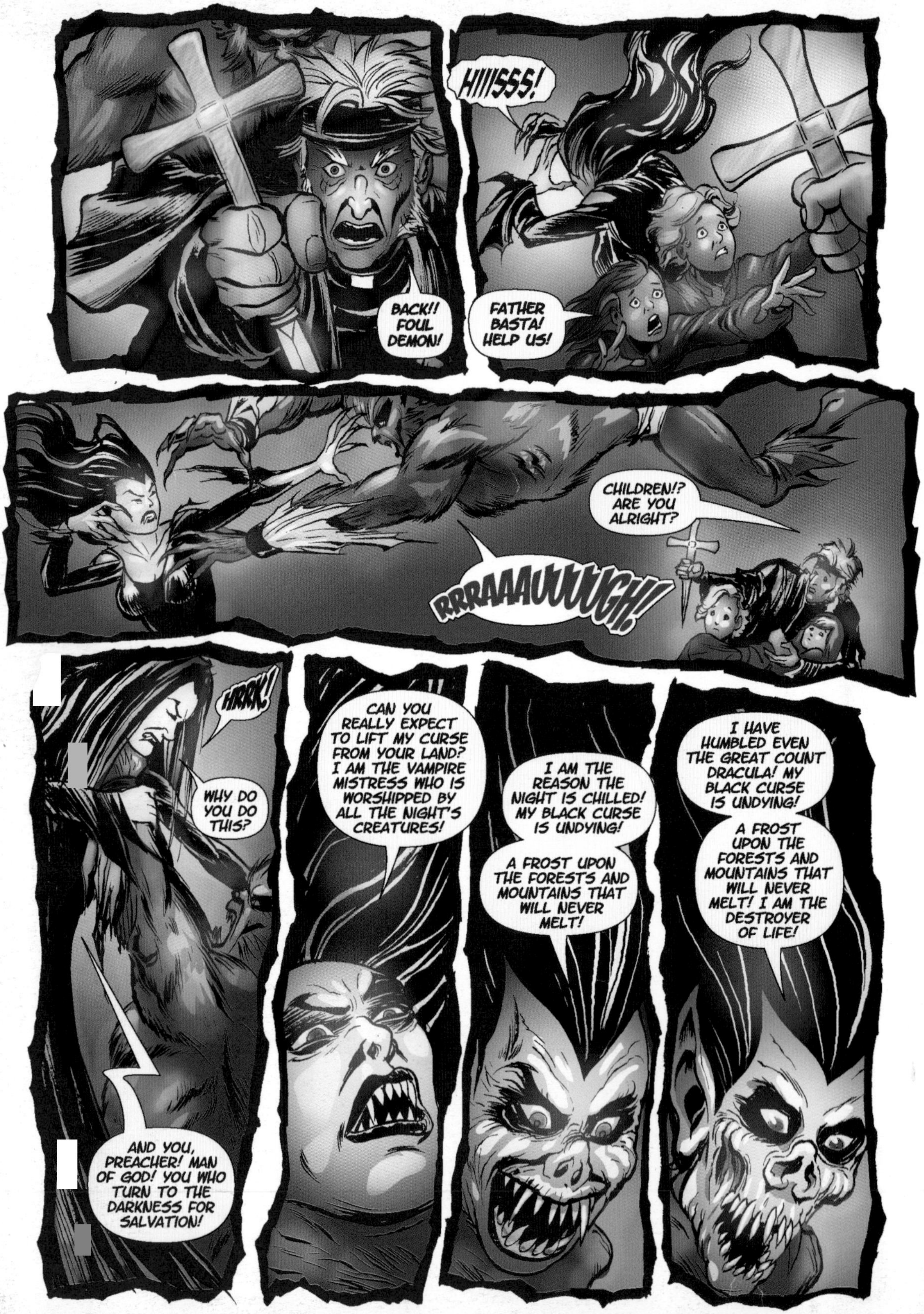
BACK!! FOUL DEMON!
HIIISSS!
FATHER BASTA! HELP US!
CHILDREN!? ARE YOU ALRIGHT?
RRRAAAUUUUGH!!
HRRK!
WHY DO YOU DO THIS?
AND YOU, PREACHER! MAN OF GOD! YOU WHO TURN TO THE DARKNESS FOR SALVATION!
CAN YOU REALLY EXPECT TO LIFT MY CURSE FROM YOUR LAND? I AM THE VAMPIRE MISTRESS WHO IS WORSHIPPED BY ALL THE NIGHT'S CREATURES!
I AM THE REASON THE NIGHT IS CHILLED! MY BLACK CURSE IS UNDYING!
A FROST UPON THE FORESTS AND MOUNTAINS THAT WILL NEVER MELT!
I HAVE HUMBLED EVEN THE GREAT COUNT DRACULA! MY BLACK CURSE IS UNDYING!
A FROST UPON THE FORESTS AND MOUNTAINS THAT WILL NEVER MELT! I AM THE DESTROYER OF LIFE!

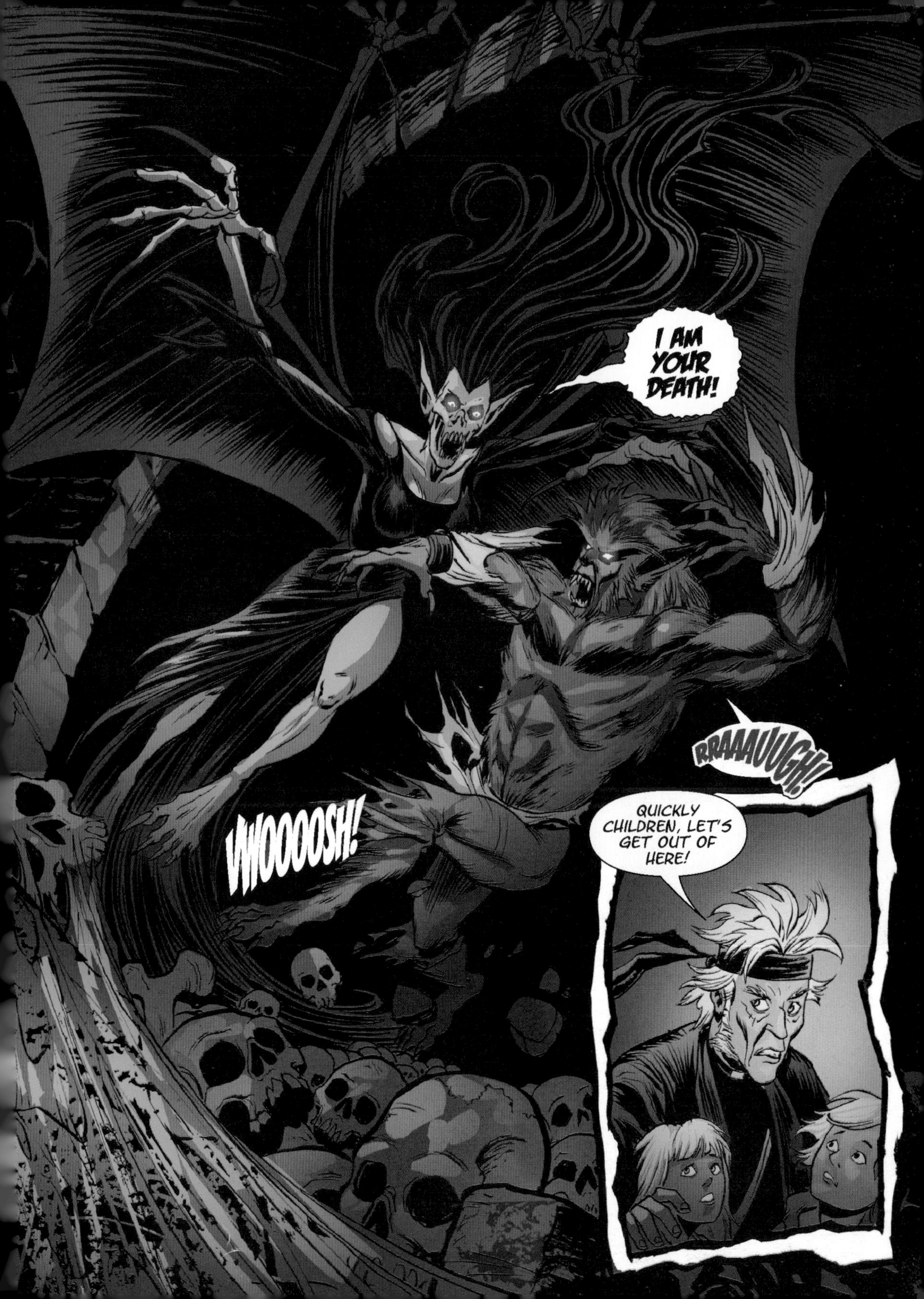
I AM YOUR DEATH!
RRAAAUUGH!
VWOOOOSH!
QUICKLY CHILDREN, LET'S GET OUT OF HERE!

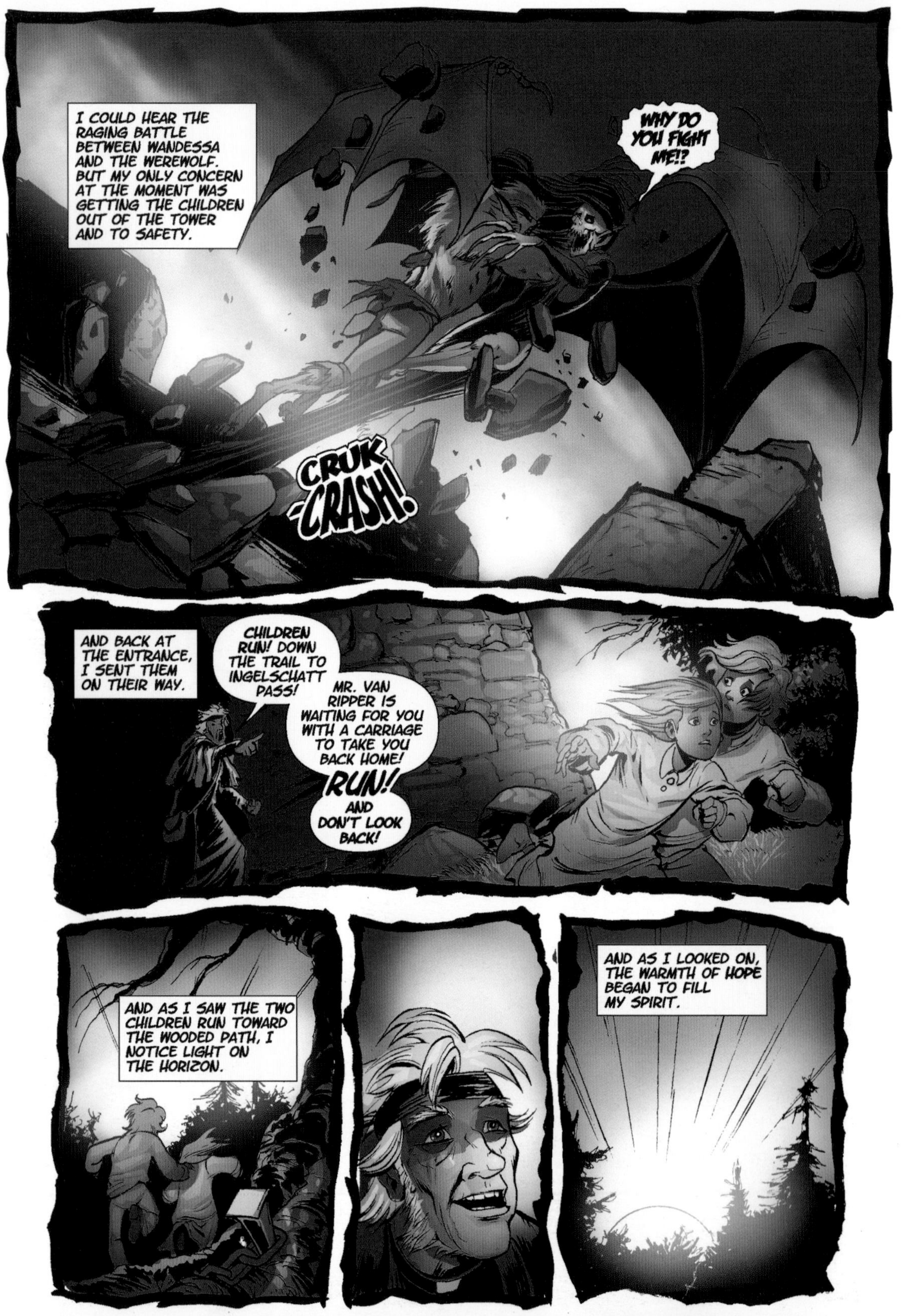
I COULD HEAR THE RAGING BATTLE BETWEEN WANDESSA AND THE WEREWOLF. BUT MY ONLY CONCERN AT THE MOMENT WAS GETTING THE CHILDREN OUT OF THE TOWER AND TO SAFETY.
WHY DO YOU FIGHT ME!?
CRUK -CRASH!
AND BACK AT THE ENTRANCE, I SENT THEM ON THEIR WAY.
CHILDREN RUN! DOWN THE TRAIL TO INGELSCHATT PASS!
MR. VAN RIPPER IS WAITING FOR YOU WITH A CARRIAGE TO TAKE YOU BACK HOME!
RUN!
AND DON'T LOOK BACK!
AND AS I SAW THE TWO CHILDREN RUN TOWARD THE WOODED PATH, I NOTICE LIGHT ON THE HORIZON.
AND AS I LOOKED ON, THE WARMTH OF HOPE BEGAN TO FILL MY SPIRIT.

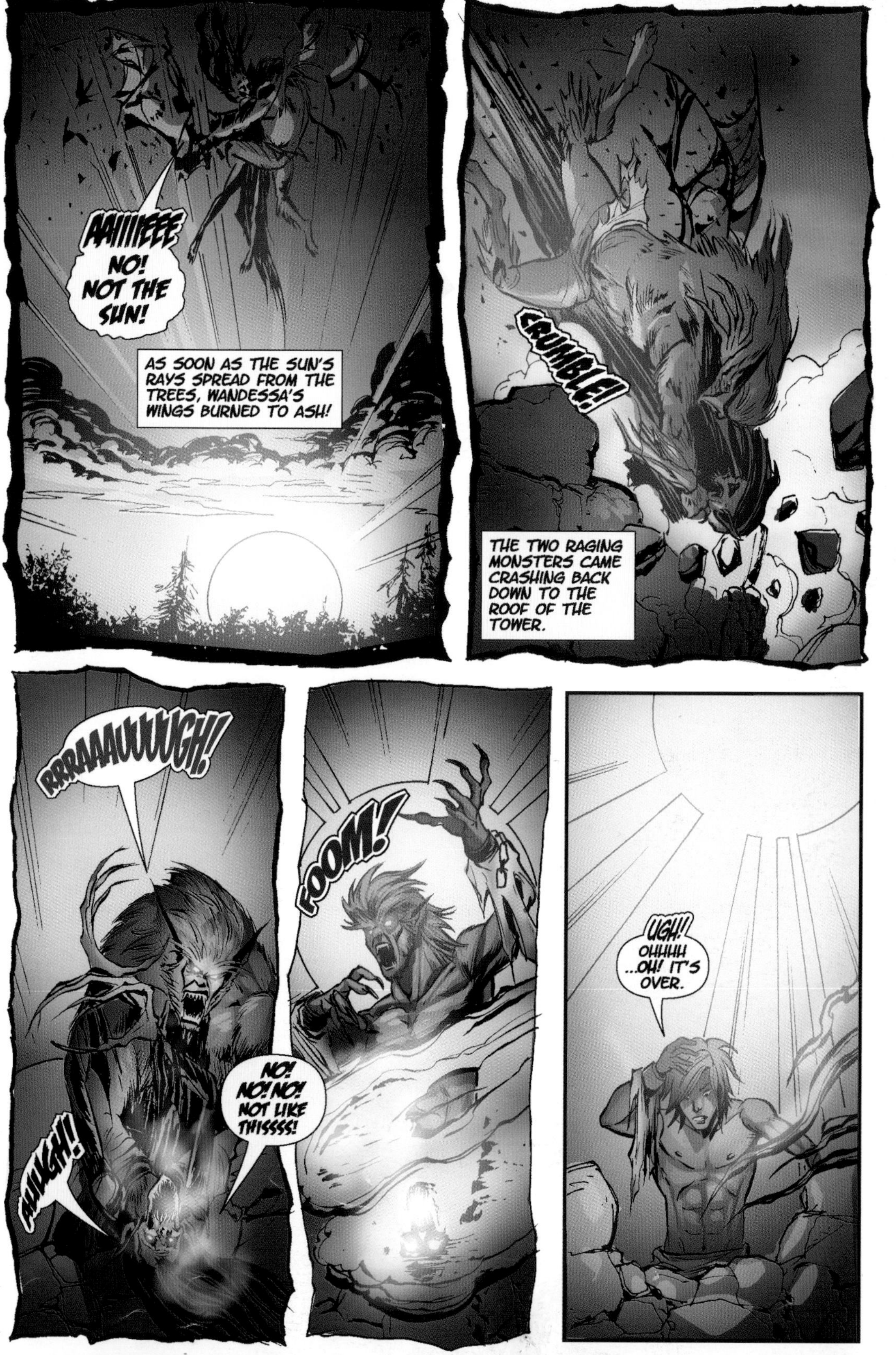
AAIIIIEEE NO! NOT THE SUN!
AS SOON AS THE SUN'S RAYS SPREAD FROM THE TREES, WANDESSA'S WINGS BURNED TO ASH!
CRUMBLE!!
THE TWO RAGING MONSTERS CAME CRASHING BACK DOWN TO THE ROOF OF THE TOWER.
RRRAAAUUUUGH!!
FOOM!
NO! NO! NO! NOT LIKE THISSSS!
AUUGH!
UGH! OHHHH ...OH! IT'S OVER.

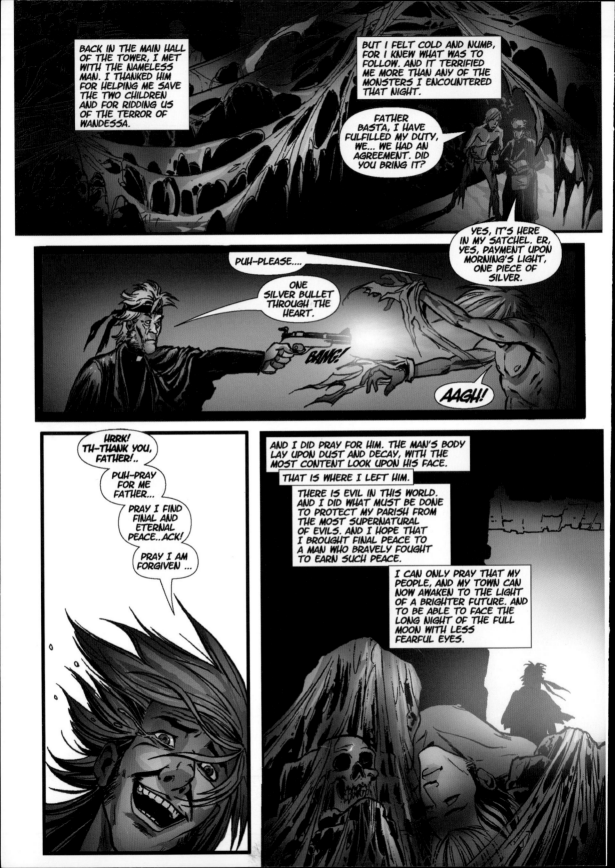

BACK IN THE MAIN HALL OF THE TOWER, I MET WITH THE NAMELESS MAN. I THANKED HIM FOR HELPING ME SAVE THE TWO CHILDREN AND FOR RIDDING US OF THE TERROR OF WANDESSA.

BUT I FELT COLD AND NUMB, FOR I KNEW WHAT WAS TO FOLLOW. AND IT TERRIFIED ME MORE THAN ANY OF THE MONSTERS I ENCOUNTERED THAT NIGHT.

FATHER BASTA, I HAVE FULFILLED MY DUTY, WE... WE HAD AN AGREEMENT. DID YOU BRING IT?

YES, IT'S HERE IN MY SATCHEL. ER, YES, PAYMENT UPON MORNING'S LIGHT, ONE PIECE OF SILVER.

PUH-PLEASE....

ONE SILVER BULLET THROUGH THE HEART.

BANG!

AAGH!

HRRK! TH-THANK YOU, FATHER!..

PUH-PRAY FOR ME FATHER...

PRAY I FIND FINAL AND ETERNAL PEACE...ACK!

PRAY I AM FORGIVEN ...

AND I DID PRAY FOR HIM. THE MAN'S BODY LAY UPON DUST AND DECAY, WITH THE MOST CONTENT LOOK UPON HIS FACE.

THAT IS WHERE I LEFT HIM.

THERE IS EVIL IN THIS WORLD. AND I DID WHAT MUST BE DONE TO PROTECT MY PARISH FROM THE MOST SUPERNATURAL OF EVILS. AND I HOPE THAT I BROUGHT FINAL PEACE TO A MAN WHO BRAVELY FOUGHT TO EARN SUCH PEACE.

I CAN ONLY PRAY THAT MY PEOPLE, AND MY TOWN CAN NOW AWAKEN TO THE LIGHT OF A BRIGHTER FUTURE. AND TO BE ABLE TO FACE THE LONG NIGHT OF THE FULL MOON WITH LESS FEARFUL EYES.

History of the Werewolf

Werewolves are the second most popular horror character after the vampire. They have been featured in myths, stories, and films for centuries. There is even a psychiatric condition where people believe they are werewolves, it is called lycanthropy. In Greek, *lykos* means "wolf" and *anthropos* means "man."

Werewolves are believed to exist in prehistoric times. In Greek, Roman, and Norse mythology, werewolves were men who changed into wolves by magic spells or herbs. They were written about by the Greek historian Herodotus and the Roman poet Virgil.

The myths spread to Europe during the middle ages. There, French laws expelled werewolves from the country. English, German, and Russian peasants also had tales of men turning into wolves.

Today, werewolves can be found in modern fiction. Horror tales are told of men bitten by a werewolf that change against their will at the time of the full moon. They devour animals and people but return to human form during the day. In many stories, a werewolf cannot die, though in the Hollywood versions of the myth it can be killed with a silver bullet.

In 1933, Guy Endore wrote *Werewolf in Paris*, which inspired films such as *The Wolf Man*. More recently, J.K. Rowling included werewolves in the Harry Potter series. R.L. Stine and Stephen Cole have also produced books about the mysterious creature. These stories and many others will help the werewolf continue to be a popular character.

Glossary

arachnid - an order of animals with two body parts and eight legs.

composure - a calmness of mind or appearance.

cult - a system of religious beliefs and customs.

inhabit - to live in or occupy a region. A place where nothing lives is uninhabited.

parish - a local church community.

rabid - having a sickness of warm-blooded animals that causes abnormal behavior and increases saliva, often leading to death.

salvation - being saved from destruction, failure, or evil.

sentinel - a guard watching a gate or entrance.

somber - serious.

Web Sites

To learn more about werewolves, visit ABDO Publishing Company on the World Wide Web at **www.abdopublishing.com**. Web sites about werewolves are featured on our Book Links page. These links are routinely monitored and updated to provide the most current information available.